Short Stories & Fragments from the Other Side

Christopher Ammann

Copyright © 2020 Christopher Ammann

All rights reserved.

ISBN: 9798675730964

DEDICATION

For my Mom, who was, and is, the best ever. For my wife, Jeanette, for picking up the pieces and always being on my side.

CONTENTS

	FORWARD	i
1	A FAMILIAR VOICE	1
2	EYE CANDY	9
3	THE KOREAN SOLUTION	12
4	THUMP	17
5	IT'S WHAT'S FOR DINNER	51
6	BUNKER LIFE	60

FORWARD

I am a book and short story writer specializing in out-side of the box sci-fi with plenty of thrillers and suspense. I have published two short stories: "Life without Power" and "Tales of the Outbound" look for them online at Amazon. You can follow me on Facebook at A Look Inside My Mind.

A FAMILIAR VOICE

Ted West walked around his latest invention with pride. It looked so deceptively simple from the outside - a ten-foot round, three-foot-high platform with a single set of four stairs leading to the top of the ring. Yet under the hood was a maze of coils and computers controlling everything. Because what Ted West had invented was a time-machine.

Circled around the ring were twelve semi-truck trailers full of generators and control rooms. Feeding the ring the power it needed to run the coils under the ring. The coils had the power to bend space-time for the lucky few standing on the ring. Anyone watching from outside would only see people on the ring. But the people on the ring would see a completely different time and space. And not only could they see it, but they could also photograph it as well! Sound and all. In testing in Maryland, it found a Native American tribe from 1000 AD that had never been seen before.

But testing was done, and now Ted and his team were going first to Italy and then on to Egypt to see how some of the wonders of the world had been built.

At dawn, Ted West and his team walked into the Coliseum in Rome and looked around in amazement at the ancient walls bathed in the morning light. Ted had handpicked the best (in his opinion) for every position. For roadies to load the trucks, he picked the best from bands like Dave Mathews and Further.

For scientific and computer expertise, Ted called old friends and asked each for who they thought was the best in the field he needed. He never looked at resumes or Linked-in to make his picks. What this gave Ted was a team he felt could do the impossible. And time travel was high on the impossible list.

As the whole team walked into the Coliseum, Layla Anderson, a roadie, was the first to speak, "We will need to set the ring higher than that first ring of seats - otherwise we will be below the original floor." Donnie Willis, a systems control specialist, followed, "And we will want the power and control leads to come over the top of whatever structure we build to raise the ring. We don't need any cables crossing in the way to the ring from the trucks."

And so, it went for the next hour till everyone's input was given and accepted. Ted West took a last look around the Coliseum and said, "Let's go see history, people!"

The convoy of trucks for the ring pulled up three rows deep to the gate where miles of the cable would be run into the Coliseum. At the same time, two other trucks were being unloaded on the other side of the Coliseum. The scaffolding went right inside and was put in place immediately. The scaffolding would hold the ring above the floor level of the Coliseum. No sooner were those trucks unloaded and moved away, two more trucks took their place. These trucks held the ring.

Back on the other side, truck doors were open, and cables were being pulled in the direction of the scaffolding. Great care was being taken to align and label every cable. Each end on the truck side was plugged into a power panel inside the trailer. Then cables were run from the panels outside the control trailers to the generator trucks. Each connection was checked and re-checked. After all that was completed, the team in the control trailers started their diagnostics programs and looked at readouts. All this without the ring being hooked up yet. After the ring was hooked up, a whole new round of diagnostics would be run. And only after all that was done, the calibration of the ring would begin.

Back inside the Coliseum, parts of the ring were being lifted into place on the scaffolding. Safety nets were hung around the scaffolding to catch anyone who might fall off the ring when it was running. This had happened a few times in testing as the view in time presented to the people on the ring was so real, anything coming at the ring looked like it would collide with those on the ring. This would cause people to jump off where they promptly found themselves right back in today. Of course, they had never really left today. They had only been allowed to look into a window of the past wrapped around the ring.

Now four hours into the set up at the Coliseum, Ted West met with his ring team. These were the people who would be standing on the ring with him. In the meeting room at the back of Control Trailer One were Mike Lefoot, Jane Freemon, and Ema Wake. All had been selected the same way Ted picked all his teams - by a combination of recommendations and face to face meetings. Everyone agreed face to face was by far the most grueling interview any had been through. Ted ran through the team in his mind. Fifty-five-year-old Mike was Ted's logistics guy responsible for getting all the gear and people to where they need to be. He is also an expert in all things ancient Rome and the Middle East. And that is why Mike was on the team because they all had many roles to fill. Thirty-four-year-old Ema was Ted's pick for an ancient language expert. Being from Eastern Europe, she had done some of the most groundbreaking research to date on dead languages. She was also a communications expert. And then there was Jane. Jane was Ted's right hand. Her true expertise was in high power magnetic fields (the very thing that made the ring work), but she also was a very accomplished physicist to boot.

Ted kicked off the meeting, "Things look to be going well with the setup guys, so let's review what we hope to see today." Mike answered, "Well, the dream is we see a full-on event complete with gladiators and a packed Coliseum." Jane jumped in. "And let's not forget we want to document the sunscreen working at the top of the Coliseum. Up until now, it had all been conjecture on how it worked and even what it looked like." Ema said, "Well, hopefully, we can record some people talking as well. That would be huge!" "Agreed," said Ted, and he continued, "Ok, let us split up and make the rounds with the setup and meet back here in one hour." And, with that, they all left the room to see about a date with history.

Ted's ring team was back in the control room after the setup inspection. They all agreed everything looked good. So, Ted pushed back from the table, looked over at Donnie in the control room, and said, "Donnie, we are a go for ring calibration." Donnie spun around and said, "Roger, that boss!" Donnie then grabbed his radio and keyed the mike, "Go for ring calibration." A voice shot back, "Underway." And, with that, cables were attached to the ring, and diagnostics run. Generators could be heard coming up to full power, and the radio came to life with calls of all systems go. After what felt like a lifetime, Donnie called back to the ring team at the back of the control room and said, "All systems go. Waiting on you, boss." Ted West looked at the team and said, "Time to fly, folks!" And they walked out of the control room and into the daylight. They passed through the gate and walked up to the platform holding the ring. One by one, they climbed to the top and took the steps up onto the top of the ring.

Everyone on the ring team wore a custom-designed video cam on their heads, recording everything they saw and heard. There was no live feedback to the control room because, once the ring went live, no signal could penetrate the wall of magnetism that would engulf the ring.

Ted keyed the radio and said, "Control ready to view." Donnie came back and said, "Roger, boss, here we go. See you when you get back." And with that, Donnie pushed the four slide bars in front of him to the top of the control panel. The generators strained to max power, and the ring began to hum. The monitor on Donnie's control panel showing the ring with the team on it went to snow white.

The ring team stood on the ring and felt the ring start to pulse as the hum turned to a roar. And then it happened. A curtain of small beads of light shot up from the ring all around them. It went up as far as the eye could see, and the curtain grew thicker with each passing second. Then the curtain of light started to take on color. Slowly at first, but then it became a flood of color. Ted would describe it later as being trapped in a rainbow. Then the curtain stopped moving, and the waves of energy that had been bouncing off the team stopped at the same instance. Then, as if a light switch had been thrown, the Coliseum was all around them. Everyone was aw struck at the sight of a complete Coliseum. And it was full to the top with people all yelling. It became clear then the event unfolding was the cause of that yelling. The floor of the Coliseum had been flooded, and a large naval war scene was playing out as one ship prepared to board the other. The ships rowed at full speed and turned hard left, heading right at the ring team. And just as the boarding started, they rowed right through the ring. Instinctively they all ducked and then laughed as the ships passed by. The boarding party, with their swords at the ready, jumped as one over to the other ship. And then the killing began. The crew of the ship being boarded could not fight back as on closer inspection, it was obvious, they were all chained to the oars. The sound from the spectators was deafening and only stopped when the last crew member was dead. And then, as on cue, two small boats came and towed the dead ship behind the winning boat for a victory lap of sorts around the Coliseum lake. Then the small fleet moved off to the side, and flood gates were opened. The water rushed away along with the ships. And before all the water was out, crews of men carried wood planks out by the hundreds. Within minutes had laid down a floor where before only water was.

The stage was now set for the next drama to be played out, and it did not take long to see what that drama would be. Five men were pushed out to the center of the Coliseum floor. On the shirt of each man, front and back, was the sign of the cross.

The five men were left alone in the middle of the Coliseum floor. With nowhere to run, apparently, guards were not needed. We looked around the Coliseum, taking tons of pictures of every detail. And this included the sun awning at the very top of the Coliseum. It was an engineering marvel. The complexity of the awning would take engineers years to figure out. Massive beams unfolded three deep to reach out to the center of the Coliseum. Then sails were unfolded out to the very end of the rigging. It was amazing.

After a few minutes, the door from which the five Christians were dragged out opened, and the crowd instantly went into a frenzy. And then a huge gladiator emerged from the shadows into the light of the Coliseum. He was easily over six feet tall and well over two hundred pounds. He carried five small swords under one arm and a shield along with a classic Roman combat sword in the other arm as if they weighed nothing at all. The gladiator marched with a very deliberate stride up to the five Christians and dropped the five small swords down in front of the men. He then placed his shield on his left arm and the sword in his right hand. The Christians did not move to pick up the swords. The gladiator, with the crowd still screaming, did not give the men a second chance. He walked up to the kneeling men. They looked up at him as they made the sign of their new religion on their chests (the cross), and without any further hesitation, one by one, the gladiator separated the men's heads from their bodies. The gladiator turned to salute the crowd, and then it happened -the Coliseum melted away, leaving only what we see today.

Ted looked at his team, and the smiles said it all. They had done the impossible and seen history. In the days that followed, they released much of the video to the academic and media outlets. The result was overnight, Ted and his team become rock stars. And when it was disclosed that the next stop was the great pyramids of Egypt, the media frenzy went into overdrive.

    The team had packed up quickly and boarded a transport ship for Egypt. The ship had no sooner left Italy when Mike came on to the bridge where the rest of the ring team was getting the star treatment from the captain. Ted saw the look in Mike's eye and said, "Hey Mike, what's going on?" Mike said, "We have a problem. The Egyptian Minister of State for Antiquities Affairs that used to be called the Minister for Antiquities Affairs, run by Zahi Hawass, took our twenty thousand for the permit to set up at the pyramids without any questions. But now that news is out that we can go back in time, it appears the price for the permit is now twenty million!" Ted's blood boiled. Ted looked over at the captain and said, "Change of plans, captain. We are going to Israel!" Ted looked at the team and continued, "We have multiple permits in Israel and the Gaza Strip. We will start at the port of Haifa. One the oldest known, going back over 3000 years. But the target time will be the same as the Coliseum setup." Jane jumped in, "Well, since we are going to be in a place that old, I think we should push in just a little deeper time-wise. I mean, what could it hurt to be in town at the time of Christ?" Ema spoke, "OMG, that is brilliant, Jane!" Mike looked around and said, "You two do realize the chance of us setting up where Christ is would be, in a word, slim." Ted said, "Point taken, Mike, but I have to agree with the Ladies on this one. I will get with Donnie and go over the changes to the timeline setup."

    They sailed into Haifa before dawn and were greeted by a crowd of over one thousand people. Most just smiled and waved, but some held signs saying everything from "Take me with you!" to "Please find my parents making love in 1957 and stop them! I don't want to be here!" It was a circus of the first magnitude. The police pushed the crowd back, and the trucks rolled off the ship into the county side. They drove onto Mount Carmel from the southwest. Working their way up the sloping grade gradually up towards the top but stopping halfway up to the 1810ft summit. Even from here, they could look out over farms in the plain below. It didn't take much imagination to think that this very much how it looked 2000 years ago. "Well, this place looks as good as any. Let's start here." Ted said over the radio. And, with that, the convoy circled the wagons and started the setup. The lot they were on was a small, flat, one-acre plot with a small rock outcropping at one end. It was next to this outcropping that the ring was set up.

The setup went smoothly, and in just three hours, the team was on the ring, ready to go. Again, Ted keyed the radio and said, "Control ready to view." With a steady voice, Donnie came back with his now-famous line, "Roger boss, here we go. See you when you get back." And, with that, Donnie once again pushed the four slide bars in front of him to the top of the control panel. Again, the generators strained to max power, and the ring began to hum. And again, the monitor on Donnie's control panel showing the ring with the team on it went to snow white.

The ring team stood on the ring and felt the familiar pulse of energy as the hum turned to a roar. Then the curtain of small beads of light shot up from the ring all around them again. Then the curtain of light took on color and then a flood of color. Then as before, the curtain stopped moving, and the waves of energy that had been bouncing off the team stopped. Then, that moment, when it's as if a light switch had been thrown, the field appeared all around them, and the field was full of perhaps forty people from 2000 years ago. And sitting on the rock outcropping right next to the ring was a man speaking to the crowd. All eyes were on the man as he spoke. No one moved a muscle as he clearly had their undivided attention. He was speaking in Hebrew, and Ema began to translate his words for the team.

As the man spoke, his voice was calm and reassuring. It reminded Ted of the way his favorite uncle would talk to him as a child when he gave him advice. Ema struggled to make out what the man was saying. She closed her eyes and raised her palm as if to hear better or to stop the other team members from saying anything. Then she started, "It's Hebrew, but it's not. It's so different. He is telling them the way. The way to his father. I think?" And just then, the man stopped talking and looked over at the ring team. He was just slightly higher than the ring standing on the rock. His eyes locked on each one at a time, and afterward, each would say it was as if he could see clear through to their souls. He then said in perfect English, "Peace be with you, my brothers and sisters. May you find my peace within yourselves. I have waited for you. Man has always struggled with good vs. evil. But fear not for evil will not win the day. When you return home, you must tell the people that the Father loves them all. But there is no place for hate in the name of the Father. All things will return to what they were in the beginning, but love because love is the true force and the only true way to the Father. Many things have changed since my time on earth, but God has not. Search for the way to Him inside each of you, and you will be shown the way. Your lives have now been forever changed because of this meeting, and the work you must take on will be with you till your last days. Remember, I am always with you." And He started to turn away, but Ted said, "What work? What are we supposed to do?" The man turned one last time to them and said, "You will teach a new man to lift up the downtrodden, you will teach new man to feed the hungry, you will teach new man to love God over material wealth, you will teach new man the way. All you need to know is inside each of you. I have seen it. Now go, and peace be with you." And, with that, He turned back to the people in the field and continued His sermon. The people looked confused now as he had been speaking in a strange tongue to no one.

And then it happened, there was a flash, and they were back. They looked at each other, and Ema said it first "That voice, I can't put my finger on it, but it was…" and they all said as one – "so familiar."

EYE CANDY

The late thirty-something, brown-haired female in a light summer dress with small flowers weaved into her braids, walked up to the house, and removed her designer sunglasses. She pulled open the screen door and walked in. A quick glance around, and she saw him right where she thought he would be, at the hundred-year-old, round, oak table with claw feet. She rushed over and sat down next to him. The only things on the table were a large yellow writing pad, a pencil, and a half-full short glass of whiskey. She said, "It's a little early for whiskey, isn't it?" "Probably," came his reply. "The writer," she thought, "always with so few words." And she continued, "Do you have it?" He answered, "Yes, but I am not sure you want to take this one." She shot back, "Why do you think I came here? Of course, I want it." "Very well then," the writer said, and he slid the pad across the table. She grabbed the pad and started to read.

She got up from the table and walked over to the door leading to the basement. She slowly turned the knob and pulled the door open. Instantly a rush of wind shot out, and the screen door behind her slammed open and shut in the wind. She looked back at the writer, but he was gone. Only the glass of whiskey remained. She turned back to the stairs and started down. The light was dim and coming from the bottom of the steps. But she could make out the stone walls and arched ceiling overhead. It all was very much out of place.

The center of the steps had a dip cut in them from centuries of foot traffic, and the light below grew brighter. She reached the bottom of the steps and was greeted with a small ten-foot by ten-foot room. Ahead of her was an iron gate and to her right was a three-foot-high handrail with an arch cut out of the stone over it. She walked over to the rail and looked down.

Inside was a beautiful spiral staircase cut out of the rock. Torches lit the way down as far as she could see. She picked up a rock and tossed it down. After a few seconds, a splash told her water was at the bottom. She had to see it. Turning her attention to the gate, she first pushed and then pulled, and to her surprise, the gate swung open.

Starting down, she could not help but be astonished at the work that had gone into the staircase. It was like one huge sculpture carved out of the earth. The same handrail and arch she had found at the top were repeated over and over every ten feet as she moved down. Then she saw ropes and buckets moving up one line and down another. "How odd," she thought. And that is when she heard the clomp, clomp, clomp of a horse.

As she came around a turn, she found herself on a platform with a horse pulling a large wooden gear around. As the horse pulled, the buckets of water went up and came back empty. As the horse showed no interest in her, she continued down the staircase. And here, things got tricky. This part of the staircase was much older and not in good repair. She had to stay too far left just to continue because many of the arches and rails had fallen away over time. And some of the steps were no longer there at all. But as she slid down one last set of what used to be steps, she was rewarded with a beautiful sight.

A smooth rock ledge that went out into a small pool of water. A small waterfall could be heard somewhere off to the right and at the end of the ledge was a girl. Dressed much like she was, she walked up to her, and they just stood and took it all in. After some time, the girl said, "The writer never disappoints in his journeys," And just then, a rock came down from above and shattered the water's surface.
Startled, she pushed back and found herself back at the oak table, his pad still in her hand. She picked up his pencil and scribbled a thank you

note below the story. She notices a similar note had already been added at the top of the page. She placed the pad down, reached into her pocket, and placed a hundred-dollar bill under the pad. Looking around and not seeing the writer, she took the half-empty glass of whiskey and tossed it down. As she headed for the screen door, she passed the door to the basement. She thought about opening it but continued, put on her designer sunglasses, and walked outside. There, to her right, was a small water feature. It was made to look like the water was coming from a stone trough coming out of the wall of the house.

THE KOREAN SOLUTION

The USSN Seawolf class submarine glided to a stop just 500 yards from the west coast of North Korea. They were southeast of Cheolsan, just north of a small bay at the tip of a nondescript peninsula. It was 01:30 and high tide, giving the special project submarine 75 feet of water. The Seawolf class is an attack-type submarine. But this one had been modified to do much more. During the Cold War, subs like this had completed missions right under the noses of the soviet navy.

The Captain asked sensors if they were clear. Sensors reported they were, but the North Korean patrol boat was still doing circles about ten miles away. The patrol boat had got a whiff of them coming in and was tearing up some sea looking for the ghost she had bumped into. "Very well," the Sipper said, "Commence operation." And, with that, a team of six highly-trained Navy Special Forces divers entered the dive chamber. After the first hatch was sealed, the chamber was flooded, and the team exited out the other hatch onto the back of the submarine.

In total darkness, they performed the tasks they had drilled on for a month. On the back of the sub was a twelve-foot round, 30-foot-long tube. It looked to the casual observer to be some type of buoy mounted on a track of some kind. After about ten minutes, the dive team leader radioed in; they were ready to deploy. The skipper clicked the mic twice. The dive team, hearing that, all turned a valve in front of them. Slowly the object lifted off the back of the sub but stayed tethered to the tracks.

Then, as small green lights glowed, the whole set of tracks swung 90° out over the side of the submarine. A button was pushed, and the object was pulled out past the sub to the end of the track. From here on, the whole process was automated. The tanks at the bottom of the object slowly filled while simultaneously the bottom cleared the end of the tracks. Once the object was vertical, the whole thing sank to the bottom. The tracks were put back in place, and the dive team returned. Total time, 30 minutes.

Once inside, a quick thumbs-up from the dive team leader confirmed to the skipper what he already knew. He ordered the submarine back out the way they had come in at 12 knots. The Seawolf class submarine can do over 30 knots but make some detectable sounds doing so. At 12 knots, no one could hear them - not even that North Korean patrol boat, which was now 15 miles away.

In 10 hours, the Seawolf class submarine was well out of North Korean waters and 138 miles from the object they had left behind. The skipper set course for the south en route to western Japan.

In the dark waters, just off the western coast of North Korea, on the bottom of the bay, the object came to life. Systems came online, system checks and rechecks were performed—all with no human intervention or oversite. Then, without warning, the top blew off the object, and its true purpose became known.

Rising out of the object towards the surface came an ICBM cocooned in a huge bubble of air. It broke the surface, leaping into the air like a breaching whale. Then, just as it started to fall back to earth, its motors came to life with a thundering roar. Within seconds it is arching over North Korea, clawing at the sky.

Deep inside Cheyanne Mountain in Colorado Springs Space Command bunker, missile launch warnings from early-warning satellites started to appear. The shift commander started asking for data and course predictions.

"Confirmed missile launch" came the response from the now wide-eyed 26-year-old behind one of the computer stations. The shift commander told his communications officer to get the word out to Alaska and Seattle that there is a bird in the air. The exact tract unknown at this time but moving west to east. Origin is North Korea. This is NOT a drill! Tell them they are free to fire at will if it approaches the west coast.

News of the missile launch had just reached the two anti-missile (THAAD) sites when the shift commander's warning came in. Up and

down the line, crews scrambled to get ready to do what they had trained to do so many times. Still, it was all surreal.
In the Colorado Springs Space Command bunker, as data from satellites was confirmed, a track was firming up. Then it was confirmed. The track is consistent with an ICBM. Can now state with 96% confidence target Seattle Washington. The shift commander asked that the information be sent to the missile defense teams and to Washington DC.

It had now been some 7 minutes since the launch of the North Korean ICBM. It had 15 more minutes of flight time until it hit Seattle. At the missile defense sites, the data from the early warning satellites was now being fed to the missile intercept solution computers. Soon this would be augmented with data from many sources along with the site's own radar.

Both teams report ready, the shift commander was told. Alaska thinks Seattle has a better shot and is deferring. "That's fine," is all he said. Seattle saw they were primary and began the launch sequence. The lieutenant over the missile crew gave the command to arm missile one of the four he had ready to fire.
Then a person stepped out of the shadows of the control room and took the lieutenant by the arm, "Lieutenant, I am Colonel Zackary from missile development." The lieutenant had seen him around but had never been introduced as he was always with higher-ups. The colonel continued, "I need you to select missile three right now. I don't, we don't have time to explain, but it has all the latest and greatest upgrades".

The lieutenant looked him in the eye and nodded. "Change command, arm missile three!" His crew did as they were told and, in a matter of seconds, came back with "Missile three selected for arming, sir." "Begin automatic launch sequence and commit to master arm of missile three," responded the lieutenant.
The rest was up to the system. Hundreds of millions, if not billions, of dollars, was about to be put to the test.

Time stopped as everyone watched the system crunch impossible numbers on speed, range, and weather conditions. Then missile three leaped off the rail. "Missile 3 away!" one of the operators stated. In a low, hushed tone, "Go baby go," was all the lieutenant could say.

Colonel Zackary came alongside the lieutenant and said, "You did good, son, we'll get this." The lieutenant could only hope this man was right; because, if they missed, the thought was too much. "Alright, team, where are we?" The lieutenant asked. "On track and tracking. The bird is hunting, sir!" said one of the operators.

"Intercept in three, two, one! Radar shows confirmed kill! We got'em!" said one of the engineers as the room exploded into back-slapping pandemonium. And, with that, Colonel Zackary turned and quietly left the room.

Within minutes, the command was given to launch a counter-strike on North Korea. The effect was as predicted—mass casualties up and down North Korea. China had begged Washington not to attack, stating they would handle the rogue state, but the U.S. was having none of it.

The next day, and for the next 30 days, U.S. and South Korean forces pounded what was left of the North Korean army along the 38° parallel. With no command or control, they were taken apart bit by bit. Some North Korean units did manage to lob some artillery shells into Seoul, but that was it. The rest was just methodical killing.

In the confusion of the first 24 hours, a North Korean sub snuck out of the harbor on a one-way mission to America. The Chinese train moved across the Yalu river heading south at just ten miles an hour. The 100-car freight train, with an engine on each end, stopped every five miles and sounded its horn; then, after 15 minutes, the train would start south again. This repeated over and over until the Geiger counter strapped to the hood of the train, just in front of the engineer, hit an unsafe level. The train would then stop and start back to China doing the same as before. On the way back, people would be waiting by the tracks with some clothes all bundled together. They climb into the car and hope to find shelter and food at the other end. For the Chinese, it was better to control the influx rather than just to let the migration happen. The camps were open, but surprisingly few people had come out of the hermit kingdom.

The American unit was working a line of North Korean bunkers north of the 38th parallel when they met fierce resistance at the entrance to one of the larger ones. It took air and artillery strikes even to get the Americans into the complex. Armor was brought up, and together they fought their way in. What they found inside was amazing. A four-panel blast door was opened, revealing a tunnel and, inside, ready for combat, was row after row of Soviet and Chinese tanks. The Soviet tanks were the 1980's vintage, like the ones they used in

Afghanistan. The Chinese tanks were the new Type 99A's. But as the Americans moved back deeper into the tunnel, it quickly became a Twilight Zone moment. The further back they went, the older the tanks got. By the time they were two miles deep, they were looking at WWII T-34 Soviet tanks. One of the privates at this point said, "Geez, these guys don't throw anything away!" By this time, they had seen enough and pulled back to report the find.

The North Korean Sang-O class sub was still playing hide and seek from the American Navy as she pushed east. She had slipped out of harbor in the middle of the night. Sang-O class subs are no match for American subs. Because they are diesel-electric, when they turn off the diesel, after charging the batteries, they get very quiet. With a good sub driver or a captain at the helm, they can be difficult to find - they have proved this many times in the past. But this Sang-O had North Korea's best driver at the helm, and he was hell-bent on getting to America. He had a package to deliver.

THUMP

My story begins with me. My name is Joshua, but everyone called me Josh. And I say everyone did because most of them are now dead. But let's not get ahead of ourselves. The night that the first thump came was an early summer night like any other in central Florida. Hot and humid during the day but nice in the evening. Few, if any, noticed the shooting stars that fell that night, and I was as guilty of missing them as anyone. My saving grace was to drink way too much at my next-door neighbor's birthday party. A twist of fate that haunts me to this day. I will leave it to others to decide if it was a gift or a curse.

My eyes crack open. My mind races, and it takes a moment for me to force my surroundings to come into focus. It is just after dawn, and I am in a drainage ditch I know well that runs behind my house. The sandy five-foot-deep hundred-yard-long ditch is meant to hold storm runoff but is empty most of the time. The trees overhead look 300 feet tall as I try to focus. Looking around, I am not alone. My dog, Sugar, is standing over me, licking my face. Sugar is a black and white Australian shepherd Boxer mix I had adopted from the Human Society three years ago. Sugar is easily the smartest dog I have ever known. Easy to train and totally loving.

As I staggered to my feet, if I had been unsure, I was now totally convinced I had drunk way too much the night before. The proof of that is the company I am keeping in the ditch with me. In the ditch with Sugar and I are Turkeys, Bobcats, Coyotes, Rabbits, Goats, Squirrels,

Raccoons, Possums, Chickens, Foxes, Dogs, Cats, and too many birds to mention. All hunkered down at the bottom of this ditch like they are hiding from the devil himself. Then a light breeze flows into the ditch, and the smell hits me. It is acid-like and unidentifiable all at once. Just then, I hear the sound of hooves running flat out over the Central Florida sand; as I look in the direction of the sound, ten deer bound over the berm and dive into the ditch with us. I pause at the word "us" as it strikes me as odd (Damn, I have to stop drinking), and as my head starts to clear, I begin to wonder how predator and prey can be side by side when Sugar knocks me down. Just as I struggle to get back up, more birds by the hundreds swarm on top of us, keeping me down and filling the ditch.

Then the sound comes - a deeper and more powerful thumping sound than any sound I had ever encountered in my entire life. It races across the ditch like a hurricane for two seconds. But in those two seconds, it was clear that any life above the ditch was now dead. And at that moment, the thought of all I had known being dead above the ditch left me devastated. I did not know how I knew, but I knew. No sooner had the sound gone by than animals left the ditch. Not in a panic. But in a kind of stately procession. First, the birds flew off, and then the animals just slowly set off in different directions. Soon there was only Sugar, and I left in the ditch.

I got to my feet and looked up, and the trees still had leaves on them. How could that be? The sheer force of what had raced over the ditch should have ripped the trees bare like a hurricane. I climbed up the side of the ditch and walked into my subdivision. Other than the paper delivery guy's car in the middle of the street, everything looked normal.

I walked up to the car and noticed it's not running. "Maybe he broke down," I wonder, but he is nowhere around. I look inside the car, and that acid smell from the ditch hits me. I look at the driver's seat, and it's covered in a stinky tan slime about an eighth of an inch-thick right where the drive should be. Ok, this is not good.

Sugar and I make a beeline for our house just two doors down. The front door is locked, and I don't want to wake my girlfriend Ginger unless I have to. She's most likely not happy with me as it is. I go around back and get into the lanai. Pull-on the sliding glass door, and it opens! "Were in Sugar," I say, and I head for the master bedroom. I walk in, and Ginger is nowhere to be seen. I peek into the master bath, and she is not there. I turn around to leave, and that is when I spot the tan slime on her pillow. I pull back the covers, and her side of the bed is covered in it. My mind goes blank. When the sound raced over the ditch, I felt like the world had ended, but now I believed it.

The next few hours are a blur of Sugar and I running from house to house. Finding only puddles of tan slime, laid out like the shadows of people on the street left after an atomic bomb, in each house we got into. All they needed was the yellow chalk line of a murder scene of screaming at the top of my lungs for someone, anyone, to answer me. But no one did answer my cries.

Sugar and I were deep in the subdivision walking back to our house when it happened. The first sign that something was terribly wrong was the squirrels started diving out of trees and running away at full speed. And simultaneously, Sugar was barking and whimpering with her tail between her legs. She did not have to tell me what was about to happen.

I swept around, desperately looking for a place to hide. We were way too far from the ditch to make it back before the next Thump. And then my eye caught a squirrel run into a drainage pipe running under a driveway. Sugar and I hit the ditch at almost the same time, and she crawled in with me right behind her. It was tight but not so tight that I couldn't push in a full six feet. The sound of heavy breathing filled the pipe for what felt like an eternity. I had Sugar's ass in my face, and she had the squirrel's ass in hers. I was just about to try and back out when it came - the acid-like smell, and then the Thump. Then it passed, just like before. The squirrel ran out, followed by Sugar and then me. I was covered in mud and more than a few cockroaches, big and small. The smell of the mud was a not so pleasing mix of car oil and decaying plant matter. Sugar and I went back to the house if for no other reason than to be close to the big ditch. It had become clear we were going to need it.

As Sugar and I arrived back at the house, I take a moment to look again at the paper guy's car. It's a late 90's model black Toyota Camry. Looking inside, the back seat is full of copies of the Lakeland Ledger newspaper. But dripping over the center from the front seat is a line of tan slime. As if he must have been reaching back to get more newspapers. The car is in park and the ignition on, but the gas gauge reads empty. So, the car ran out of gas.

The paper guy comes through about 3:30 am on Sunday, so the first Thump hit around then. Sunrise was at 7:00 am, so the second Thump was around 7:15 or 7:30. The last Thump was around 3:00 pm. Not much of a pattern to go on as to when to expect the next Thump. But the good news is that cars still run. Maybe I can drive my way out? But how would I know when to pull over and take cover? There is no way I could see the signs of an impending Thump from a moving car. That would mean I would have to rely on Sugar, but even then, what if we were not near cover? I knew the answer to the last question, game over.

So, Sugar and I walk back to our house, walk through the front door I had left open in my hasty departure from that morning. I close the master bedroom door without looking in and go to the living room. I grab the phone – nothing. Same with the cell.

I pick up the DirecTV remote and press ON. Bang! CNN! And all they are talking about is the disaster in central Florida. For the next hour, it's a nonstop rush of stories about some sort of dead zone from Miami to Gainesville. And how all attempts to reach anyone in the dead zone have failed. Virtually all communication with the outside world has been cut off. And to make matters worse, a convoy of National Guard trucks went in but lost contact sometime around 3:00 pm. But before that, they reported miles of wrecked cars in both directions of I75 just north of Gainesville. The vehicles were reported empty except for some sort of tan slime. Aircraft flown in were also lost right at 3:00 pm as well, but they reported the same thing. No people were moving, and lots of wrecked cars, along with some fires.

After an hour, a report came in from the Florida Keys saying people there reported hearing a strange thumping sound overnight and into today. With the last one being at 3:00 pm. The news anchor said it was unclear if the sound was related to the current situation.

I go to the refrigerator and make a sandwich. Sugar has spent this time camped out at the master bedroom door. I put some dog food in her cup, but she does not have an appetite. And that's when the power went out. Just as well, I thought. The phones do not work, so why should the lights. The power plant down at Lake Parker was probably running on autopilot without its human masters until something happened that the computers could not deal with and shut it all down. Or, I mused, the mother ship just blew it all to hell. Either way, the lights were out.

I had been tempted to sleep inside and run to the ditch if needed. But the power going out made my decision on where to sleep really easy. With no air conditioning, Sugar and I would be in the ditch. So, I packed a backpack with some things, including clothes, rope, food, water, a cigar lighter, a knife, and a gun. I grabbed my sleeping bag and walked into the back yard, then down into the ditch.

The night came, and Sugar and I made ourselves at home in the bottom of the Big Ditch as I had so named it. Under the stars, I replayed the day's events over and over in my mind. I asked myself all the same questions I would ask when we had a problem that needed to be addressed at work "What do we know?" Well, that was easy. Everyone in central Florida, as far as I could tell, was dead. This included many animals as well as humans. Some animals can sense when a Thump is coming. And there are tons of food in homes and stores so that we won't go hungry.

As I continued, I asked, "What don't we know?" What the hell this Thump is, and where it comes from? Where is it going? This skipped over a lot of questions like why. Why do this? For what? Why, Why, Why? And finally, I asked, "What do we think we know?" We need to get out of here. But how? Wait for rescue or make a run for it. If CNN is right, the dead zone goes north of Gainesville and south to Miami. Gainesville is a 2-hour drive, and Miami is three and a half hours. So, my money was on Gainesville. If the pattern held with significant gaps in time between Thumps, I could theoretically drive it.

I take out a pad and paper and start a record of when the Thumps hit. If there is a pattern, I have to find it. And the sooner, the better. It was then that something dawned on me. There were no mosquitoes! At this time at night, I should have been sucked dry by the bastards. And then I realized that I did not hear any of the night sounds. No tree frogs, no insects, nothing. Nothing but an eerie quiet.

Sugar and I wake at dawn. It had been a Thump free night. It did occur to me that maybe the Thump nightmare could be over. I walk out of the Big Ditch and go to the kitchen to make breakfast. I fire up the grill on the lanai and scramble five eggs with some cheese and cream. The stuff in the fridge won't last long, so I cook it up.

I put some eggs on the floor for Sugar, and she gobbles it down. I am eating my eggs when the thought hits me. Why are the eggs not turned to slime? Is it just breathing animals and insects? The meat in the refrigerator looks good too many questions, not enough answers.

I finish my eggs and go to the garage. I pull out the generator we kept on hand for hurricanes and set it up outside. I run an extension cord into the house and plug in a power strip with the TV and DirecTV box.

I am just about to hit the power button when Sugar starts barking and crying! I drop the remote and sprint to the Big Ditch, with Sugar right next to me. I jump feet first into the ditch, just as a wave of wildlife does the same, and we all hit the bottom of the ditch at the same time.

Within seconds the acrid smell fills the ditch, and the Thump comes and goes. I stand up to watch the exodus of animals. To my eye, it looks like there is fewer this time. I wonder if they went somewhere else or they had been picked off. Just how long any of us could play this game before getting picked off was anybody's guess.

Sugar and I walk back to the house where the generator is still running. I walk in and fire up the TV. CNN was just playing reports of the more lost rescue teams just moments ago. Many had driven in overnight and had made it to Tampa only to find even the MacDill Air force base empty.

So, I watch until there is no more useful information. That takes about an hour. It is clear they know as much as I do or less. The theories run from some sort of Russian secret weapon (that the Russians deny) to a string of small high-altitude North Korean nukes.

I wonder why they are not talking about the tan slime and what it is, or what the sound is they keep hearing in the Florida Keys. Is it a cover-up? The panic level must be at an all-time high. But it sounds like they are going to stop sending in rescue teams for now. And are going to step up surveillance flights instead.

That will work as long as they are the pilotless kind - like a predator. I don't think the civilian type of drones has the legs for this game. Dang, day two, and we really are getting our asses kicked.
Ok, enough of this shit. It's obvious I am going to be here for some time, so it's time to get real about long term survival. I shut down the generator, grab the bathtub liner we had for hurricanes, and start filling it. That gives me twenty-nine gallons of freshwater. Who knows how long the water will stay on? So, it's time to make hay.

I grab the big trash can (the one we had to buy so the city trash truck could pick it up automatically with a mechanical arm) and wheel it over to the lanai. I take a hacksaw and cut the downspout on the gutter. I stick the end in the trash can, and voila, water catch. My neighbors have pools, but this way, I won't have to get it. And I plan to do a propane round up to keep the grill going.

It was now noon, and I was going to look around for a golf cart when Sugar started barking and crying! Once again, we run. Again, we dive into the ditch. Again, the smell comes. Again, the Thump roars. Again, we are alive.

And so, we started to settle into our new life. For right now, any thoughts of escaping north or south went out the window. There was just no telling when the next Thump was coming. In the days that followed, Thumps came at all hours of the day or night and at different intervals. One time a Thump came just a minute apart. That one almost got me.

We had just ridden out a Thump, and I started back to the house. I got to the top of the ditch and looked back to see where Sugar had gotten off to. She was still in the ditch, along with all our animal friends. They all looked at me, and I looked back at them. And then the light went on, and I dove headfirst into the ditch. The Thump was right on my heels! But where was the acrid smell? Again, too many questions and too few answers.

Over the next couple of weeks, the central Florida summer rains started in earnest, and life in the ditch was not as comfortable as it had been. The ditch could have as much as three inches of water in it, depending on the amount of rain. Luckily, the water would seep back into the sandy ground as soon as it stopped raining.

I was living on canned goods almost exclusively. Any food left in the freezers was no longer fit to eat. Some of the neighbors had gardens, but deer were grazing the neighborhood at will now, and the gardens were a favorite dining spot for them.

I would only make quick scavenging runs out into the neighborhood with Sugar. If a house had a good drainage ditch in front (something many did to move rainwater out of the neighborhood), I would take more time. If not, it was in and out, as quick as possible, using our trusty golf cart. Well, my neighbor's trusty golf cart, that is. I could have made much more progress on my survivor efforts if it wasn't for the constant fear of the next Thump. As it was, I did have plenty of food and water to flush the toilet. Like much of Florida, we used a drain field, and we're not hooked up to a sewer system. So, I flush the toilet with rainwater and drink and cook with rainwater that I boiled on the grill. My neighbors loved bottled water, so that is a huge plus.

And that was how it was for the next few weeks. Thumps came and went like rain. And I dutifully recorded each one. CNN and the world could not get a grip on what was happening here. It got to the point that I only watched TV once a day. The tan slime had hardened and then dissolved away. Even the bed where Ginger died now showed no sign of her ever being there.

But there were stranger things going on. Sometimes at night, there would be lights coming from the southeast. The only thing out that way this far South of Lakeland was highway 60 and the small city of Mulberry. But between here and highway 60 is a large wasteland five miles wide by two miles deep of old phosphate land that was never reclaimed. Wild hogs and some lakes back there, but that was it. Even trees didn't grow on that land, only grass and weeds.

Then there were the strange sounds. A swooshing sound like a basketball blasting by an inch from your ear. Sometimes it was very short in duration, and other times it would go on for a minute or more. The only constant was the sound always came from the South and sounded like it was heading off to the North West. Again, I made notes of all of this.

I had built a simple lean-to on some pallets in the Big Ditch just to make it a little more comfortable. I found I slept much better in the ditch with a roof over my head. The lean-to was made from old two by 4's and tarps - not fancy but very homeless camp sheik.

After a good night's rest with no Thumps, I loaded Sugar into the golf cart. I was going to test my observations of the Thump and make a trip I had put off as long as I could. We were going to the supermarket.

Man does not live on corn alone, that I was sure of. Odd as it may sound, most people don't keep large amounts of canned meats on hand in the pantry. And if the pattern held, a Thump-free night would most times be followed by a Thump-free morning. Well, that's what my records showed.

We blasted out on the freshly charged golf cart. The neighborhood was full of deer, and I took this as a good sign. The Publix supermarket was only half a mile away, right outside the neighborhood. We flew out of the subdivision and hung a left on to Lakelands Highlands Road. The entrance to Publix was only 1000 feet away.

I heard them a second before I saw them. Military Humvees - blasting through the intersection of 540A and Lakelands Highlands Road heading east. I started blowing the horn and flashing the lights. It was the guy in the fourth hummer that finally saw me. They all locked up the brakes at once.

The Humvee in the middle of the intersection turned on to Lakeland Highlands and raced towards us. It skids to stop just feet from us, and the doors flew open. The guy from the passenger side got out and said, "Do you know you are the first person we have seen?"

"Hell, yes!" I said as a total of three guys piled out of the Humvee, and a round of back-slapping and handshaking took place along with introductions. "I'm Josh, Josh Baker," I said to the first soldier, he responded, "Lieutenant Ben Walker, damn glad to meet you, Josh. This is Sargent Bill Smith and Private Tom Wilson. So, Josh, what in the name of sweet water is going on around here?"

We have been on the road all night from just north of Gainesville. Cut down 75 to Tampa to MacDill. Nothing and no one alive. We got orders to take 60 to Avon Park bomb range when the brass said to head here. Said the navy had triangulated the epicenter to right near here."

"I wish I knew, Lieutenant," I said and then started to tell them about how I had survived when Sugar started barking and crying. "What's wrong with your dog?' Wilson asked. "No time to explain! If you want to live, come with me!" I yelled and started running for the ditch on the side of the road.

Walker yelled, "Get him!" and Wilson and Smith raced after me as I looked for the best place in the ditch to get into. At the end of the ditch closest to Publix were a large pipe and a steep bank. Sugar went to the pipe, but it was blocked by a storm grate.

I turned around to see Walker getting on the radio of the Humvee just as the smell hit me. The same acid smell that almost always came before a Thump. Wilson and Smith jumped on top of me, tackling me and sending all three of us tumbling to the ground on the bottom of the ditch.

As we hit the ground, I did my best to keep Wilson and Smith from picking me up. Using my legs to keep the three of us knotted up together. And then it happened, just as it had done 181 times before, the Thump came.

The Thump rushed over the ditch, totally scaring the hell out of Wilson and Smith. When it ended, they both looked big-eyed at each other and then at me. "We can get up now," I said as calmly as I could. We untangled our bodies and stood up. Wilson and Smith looked over to the Humvee, and Smith called, "Lieutenant Walker, sir, where are you?" No answer. "He's gone," I said. "What do you mean he's gone?" Smith asked, "Gone where?" and with that, Wilson and Smith pushed past me and ran over to the Humvee. Of course, I knew what they would find.

Wilson and Smith reached the Humvee, only to find the radio mike sitting in a pool of tan slime that was half inside and half outside the vehicle. "What is this crap?" Smith asked, pointing to the tan slime. But before I could answer, there was an explosion coming from the direction of 540A where the other Humvee's had been.

We took off on foot across the street and ran behind the CVS store. As we rounded the corner of the store, we were between the store and the power substation. The view was not what Wilson and Smith wanted to see. The Humvee's had rolled down the hill on 540A and piled into each other at the bottom, where most of them now were on fire and cooking off ammunition.

"We got to get down there and help them," Wilson said. "There is no one to help. They all suffered the same fate as Lieutenant Walker, I am afraid. And we will too unless we get out of here." I said. "Movement, get down," Smith said in a hushed tone.

"Where?" Wilson asked as we duck behind a cement wall. "Right there at the bottom of the hill by the lead Humvee," Smith said. We ease our heads up over the wall, there at the bottom of the hill are two white and tan spheres about 3 feet in diameter. The spheres have tan stripes with some sort of symbols or writing on the sides - light pulsing from inside as they float in the air circling around the first Humvee, apparently unfazed by the ammunition that continues cooking off all around them.

Beams of light emitted from the spheres probe every inch of the Humvee. Now apparently satisfied with the inspection of the first Humvee, they move in unison on to the second.

Smith spoke again in that hushed tone, this time with more than just a hint of concern in his voice, "Gentlemen, as quietly and fast as you can fall back to our Humvee." We spun around away from the wall; on our hands and knees, we spider crawled back around the corner of the drug store; once around the corner, we shoot to our feet for the sprint to the Humvee.

At the Humvee, Smith says, "Grab as much gear as you can from the Humvee and get it on to the golf cart. We don't want to be here when those things make it to the top of the hill and see one more Humvee take a look at" It's a mix of ammo, weapons, and backpacks that make it to the golf cart. No one says a word as we jump in the cart with me driving and take off. Sugar runs alongside in a full out run as we swing back into the neighborhood.

I slow down long enough to get Sugar to jump in my lap. "Why are you stopping for the dog!?" Smith asks in a not so friendly tone, to which I respond, "This dog is the only thing keeping us alive, and we don't need her bone-tired." We fly into the garage and, without being asked, Wilson hops off the cart and pulls down the garage door. Wilson turns around from closing the door and says, "I didn't see those things crest the hill before we took the turn, so I think we are in the clear." Smith asks, "Josh, have you seen those things before?" I tell them, "The spheres? No. The Thump, every day. But the spheres do explain some of the lights and sounds I have been hearing coming from the southeast."

The four of us move into the house and continue our conversation at the kitchen table. For the next half an hour, I tell Wilson and Smith all I know about what is going on. Including showing them the pad, I keep of the time and date of each Thump. And when I'm done, I ask them, "so, you two are special forces, right?' Wilson and Smith exchange a glance and a nod before Smith says, "Yes, we are or were until most of the team met that Thump. But how did you know?" I pretend not to notice Smith is already calling it 'Thump.' "No unit patches," I tell them. "Good eyes," Smith says.

"Thanks." I respond and ask, "So what does the government know about this mess?" Smith tells me, "Not much, I'm afraid, or we would not be here. So far, three teams have gone in before us and around one hundred regular army and reserve personnel. But all have been lost." "Until now, guys, 'til now," I said.

I continue, "So where is the satellite radio? In the garage?" Smith answers, "The team only had one, and it was in the second

Humvee." I say, "Oh, the Humvee that was blowing itself to bits at the bottom of the hill?" "That very one," Smith replies. Wilson jumps in, "It's not all bad, Josh. We have a regular radio with us, and it has a range of twenty miles. We can talk, and data link to any other unit or drone that comes in range."

I was just about to inform Mr. Wilson that we were a lot more than twenty miles from anyone when some movement on the wall caught my and Smith's eye at the same time. It was some light from the outside, hitting the far wall of the kitchen and walking its way across. Smith signaled Wilson to get eyes on the front yard. He moved expertly to the window and looked out. He quickly signaled that he had eyes on two spheres moving past the house. We stayed still until the spheres had passed by and moved up the street.

"Josh, where does this street go?" Smith asks me. "It's a dead-end with a cul-de-sac," I answer. I no sooner get the words out when Smith says, "Everyone on the floor!" We hit the floor, and simultaneously the lights came back into the house, crawling the walls. We lay on the floor for a few seconds till the lights are gone. We get up off the floor in time to watch the spheres move methodically down the street. Lighting up each house as they go.

Smith spoke first, "Damn, those things could be just about anything. Reconnaissance drones, security, and perimeter defense weapons, who knows." Or a combination of all that," Wilson added. "Well, if the sounds I have heard at night have been them moving out, there must be hundreds, if not thousands, of them," I said.

Smith said, "Let's take a look at the map and see where these things could be calling home base." Smith retrieved a backpack from the garage and took out a map. I pointed out our location and could see a big red circle already on the map. Smith continued, "Now this is where command says the navy thinks the Thump is coming from," as he pointed to the circle on the map.

I was just about to tell him what was there when Sugar barked and cried at the same time. I jumped up and said, "Come on! That's the sign!" we all ran to the Big Ditch and jumped in. I guess I had become used to seeing animals of all descriptions come flooding into the ditch before a Thump because Wilson and Smith were impressed. Or perhaps they did not believe all the things I had been telling them?

The last ones to the ditch (again) were the deer. We heard their hooves pound the sand just as the acid smell reached the ditch, and then they came flying in the ditch, landing all around us. One, in particular, was just inches from Smith's face!

The deer had been in the ditch less than a second when once again, the Thump came roaring overhead. After the Thump had passed, I took a quick census of the animals left, and it was clear there were way fewer. I turned to Wilson and Smith and said, "We are missing about half of what we started with" "You're talking about animals? Right, Josh?" Smith asked. "Right," I said.

It was now after 6 pm and time for dinner. So, we walked back to the house, and I fed Sugar as we all chipped in preparing dinner. Wilson asked, "So that's how it been, huh, man? Dog barks, you run to the ditch?" I said, "Pretty much, and her name is Sugar." Wilson said, "Sorry, Josh, just asking, you know, trying to see things from your perspective." Smith chimed in, "Right, congrats on making it, Josh. Shows you got real guts. Most people would have folded." "Thanks, guys, it means a lot coming from you," I replied.

So, we sat down to a dinner of MRE's and canned vegetables; I broke out some fine Canadian whiskey (a gift generously donated by one of my neighbors) and poured us each a glass. Then with Sugar at our feet, we watched the sun go down in a blaze of color. We sat there deep in our thoughts till Smith spoke, "We are going to have our hands full in the next few days." And without another word, we got up and went to bed in the ditch.

We were only in the Big Ditch for an hour when the first Thump came. It was followed by another, and then another until a total of twelve Thumps passed in just two hours. After the fourth or fifth Thump, Smith asked if this was normal. I told him no, I had never seen this many Thumps in a row. Smith asked what I thought it meant. "Anything, nothing, take your pick," I responded.

In the morning, we went back to the house and started pouring over the maps in earnest. Smith explained how they were moving towards Crews Lake Road to find a road onto the old phosphate land where the navy thought the Thumps were coming from before spotting me.

I told them Crews Lake Road did border the north side of the phosphate land, but we had access right here at the end of Lakeland Highlands. The Scrub Oak preserve there only had a chain-link fence separating it from the phosphate land.

Smith asked if the Scrub Oak preserve had good cover to hide our movements. I told Smith and Wilson it had the only cover. It was the only unmined land that far south. After that, it is all wasteland as far as the eye can see. Does it have a ditch we can use? Smith asked. Only one, and it's right where the old railroad tracks go into the phosphate land. I told Smith.

Well, what about this rail line here? Wilson asked, pointing to the tracks shown on the map as running behind the Big Ditch. It's just a footpath now till you get back to the phosphate lands, and then it has tracks again. The tracks outside had been taken up years ago.

Wilson asked if I had ever been on the phosphate land. I told him no, but I had gotten a pretty good look at it on my many trips to the Scrub Oak preserve with Sugar. Good enough to know where the good ditches are? Smith asked. No, not a chance. I said. Then Smith brought up the obvious, "You know Josh, we need you to come with us on this. It's your neck of the woods; Sugar is your dog, and when we go in, no matter what we find, chances are we could be in for a fight."

I told Wilson and Smith I had planned all along to go. "Hell," I said. "What else am I going to do? Hide in this damn ditch the rest of my life!" The three of us busted out laughing, and that was that. We were going in.

We spent the rest of the day inventorying everything we had grabbed off the Humvee. As for weapons, it worked out to be four M16's with 500 rounds, six pistols of mixed calibers (9mm and 45), and 200 rounds of each pistol caliber. A pretty sad total for starting a war with an unknown enemy.

Smith looked at the meager collection and said, "We have to risk a trip back to the Humvees and load up on weapons." Wilson and I looked at each other, and Wilson said, "Not sure that's such a good idea, boss. The spheres looked them up and down. How do we know it's not a trap now?" Then I said, "Well, before we go anywhere, I have a few questions. You guys must have got some images of what is out there. Satellite or drone, something. So, what did it show? What are we up against?"

Smith looked at Wilson and said, "Show him," and without a word, Wilson reached into the map case and pulled out some glossy photos. "This is all we have," Wilson said at last. I pour over the photos and what is evident right away is that most of the old phosphate land is not clear. It looks like it has all been blurred out.

"Is this the best we got?" I ask. "Not only can't you see any detail but looking at the time stamp here, this is a week old." Smith answered, "The best and brightest don't have a clue about who, what, or how this is happening. But every attempt to put sensors on this spot of the earth has failed."

Just then, the radio beeps. Wilson flips the antenna up in one smooth motion and pulls down a small keyboard from the front of the radio. He types in a few characters and proclaims, "We got a sat link via a drone." Smith said, "Send the SITREP," to which Wilson replied, "SITREP uploaded and confirmed."

I was wondering when they had put together the situation report they had just sent and what was in it when Wilson yelled out, "New mission pack coming in. They want us to stay put and wait for a new mission plan. And they want Josh's date of birth and SS number." I tell Wilson my date of birth and my social and watch as he keys it in. Wilson then collapses the antenna and puts the radio down on the floor.

I ask Wilson, "Wow, what was up with wanting my info?" Wilson answers, "I don't know, but it sounds to me like you either just got top-secret clearance or drafted," and with that, Smith and Wilson burst out in laughter. I continue, "Ok, so if you don't mind me asking, what was in the SITREP?" Smith looked at Wilson and gave him the nod. Wilson picks up the radio and flips out the keyboard, and the screen behind the keyboard comes to life. Wilson put the radio on the table and turns the screen in my direction. "Have at it," Wilson said.

My eyes adjust to the screen, and there it is. A minute by minute account from the time they left north Florida until the time they encountered me. From that point on, they had placed every detail I had told them as to how I had survived into the report. Along with supporting firsthand accounts of their encounters with the Thump. The last line of the report states, "After weighing all factors, the only known survivor's knowledge and expertise will prove invaluable going forward."

Before anyone else could say a word, the lights streaming in the windows had us diving for the floor. Smith said, "Damn, I wonder if they picked up our transmission?" Wilson replied, "If not, the timing of the spheres was impeccable." I said, "It's got to be more than two or three. Look how many lights are poking around."

Smith whispers, "Get the equipment into the laundry room, and let's get to the garage" We all gather up anything near us like guns, ammo, and backpacks. We pile it up on the washer/dryer, close the door behind us, open the door to the garage and crawl in, closing that door behind us as well.

The only light in the garage comes from a small 10-inch square window on the side door to the garage. Outside of the door is a small high fenced in area for garbage cans surrounded further in the shrubbery, making access to the window very difficult from the outside. Smith signals Wilson to take a look outside through the window. Wilson moves to the side of the door and slowly moves the right side of his face across the window. It only takes a second for Wilson to spin away from the window.

Wilson scrambles back to Smith, Sugar, and me and forcefully signals we need to get up into the attic ASAP. I look at Smith, and he nods at the rope for the pull-down ladder that leads to the attic over the garage.

That was all I needed to know. Without any additional encouragement, I slink over and pull the hatch down, unfolding the ladder as smoothly and quietly as I can. Smith goes up first and waits as I hand him Sugar and join him in the attic. Wilson is right behind me, and just as I start closing the hatch shut light fills the garage below us. The light is so intense that it looks like something right out of a horror movie. The light spills up from every crack and crevasse that is the ceiling of the garage - shifting slowly from side to side; the light becomes like an animal on a leash straining to get to us.

After what feels like a lifetime, the light disappears. But then, just as suddenly, there is a massive sound of glass shattering coming from the back of the house. As one, we all look in the direction of the sound and see the same light show coming up from the back of the house.

And this time, the light is accompanied by a sound. A low hum that vibrates into every fiber of our bodies. The light moves around the living room, and we track its progress as it moves past each light fixture and AC vent - forcing light up into the attic.

Then the light and sound gets to the door to the laundry room and stops. We hear the sound of the wood door to the laundry room cracking and straining as the light and sound gets more and more intense. Then, just when I was sure the door would explode, the light and sound drop off dramatically.

We listen as the sound fades out in the direction of the back of the house. Smith moves to the front of the attic, over the garage, where there is a hexagon-shaped vent at the peak of the roof. As he looks out the vent, he signals us to come where he is at the vent.

Wilson goes first and takes a look. He looks only for a few seconds before moving out of the way for me to have a lookout of the vent. I move up to the vent, and it takes a moment for my eyes to adjust to the daylight. But then I see what has been going on.

All around the neighborhood, Spheres by the hundreds are swarming everywhere. A longer look shows they are working in teams of five or six Spheres each and going house to house. I have a good view of the back yard of a house on the next street over.

The Spheres circle the house pouring light on and into it. Then one Sphere moves to the back sliding glass doors and begins to push on them. I could see the Sphere pulse with energy as it glows with power till the sliding glass door shatters. And when the glass shatters, the

Sphere moves immediately inside. As it does so, the remaining Spheres take up positions around the house. It was plain that this was the scene being repeated at the same time all over the neighborhood. The Spheres are looking for something or someone. And chances were, we are it.

    The reconnaissance in force, as Smith liked to call it, went on for hours as we took turns keeping watch on the proceedings from the garage vent. Then just before sunset, Wilson was at the vent when he turned and exclaimed, "They're gone! They all turned and filed out to the South East."

    Smith shot up off the floor and looked out the vent. Without missing a beat, Smith said, "Let's get back downstairs. I got a feeling we are in for a good Thumping" The words no sooner left his mouth when Sugar started to bark and whimper.

    Wilson was first to the hatch. In one swift motion, he jumped on the hatch and, as he fell, pulled the ladder out. Sugar made the floor in one leap with myself and Smith right behind her.

Sugar ran straight to the garage side door with the three of us behind her. Wilson fumbled with the deadbolt and door handle lock for only a split second before the door swung open. The four of us tumbled out onto the fenced-in area for garbage cans then made a beeline for the backyard and the safety of the Big Ditch.

    We were ten feet from the ditch when we got hit with that acid smell that almost always proceeds a Thump. Sugar flies into the ditch ahead of us like a retriever going after one of those rubber ducks they throw in the jumping competitions. The three of us fall in the ditch headfirst just as the Thump roars over us.

    I look back to see that Smith and Wilson are ok and I see Wilson's boot is way too close to the lip of the ditch. I ask Wilson, "Are you ok?" Wilson slides down to the bottom of the ditch, holding his right leg.

    Wilson, talking very fast, blurts out, "I can't feel my right foot!" Smith and I move next to Wilson and start to look him over. We gently lift his right leg and inspect his boot. Smith and I look at the boot and then look back at Wilson. Wilson asks, "Is it bad?" Smith cuts the bootstraps off, and the boot falls off in his hand. Smith holds the boot up for Wilson to see. Wilson takes one look and starts to laugh. The bottom of his boot is missing from almost everywhere but the toes.

"Wow!" Wilson finally said. "That was close." I ask, "Can you feel anything now?" Wilson moves his foot around and gives a thumbs up. I tell Wilson, "One inch more, and instead of being the first known human to survive a hit from a Thump, we would be kicking dirt on your puddle of brown crap."

Just then, another Thump rips across the sky. It passes, and Smith notes that the Thump did not have the acid smell precede it. Then Smith continues, "This is a good thing. These Thumps are the same reaction as when we first showed up. So, they are reacting to us in a way we have seen already."

Another Thump rips and then another and another in quick succession. We settle down with animals in the Big Ditch for what is sure to be a big show of power, from who or what is behind the Thump. The Thumps continued past the dawn of the next day. The last one was around nine am. We did not leave the Big Ditch until we see the animals depart. But even when the animals leave, they do not go far. Instead, they mill about not more than one hundred feet from the ditch.

Smith and I walk to the back of the house, and Wilson goes next door to look for some hunting boots. We see the damage done by the Sphere. The sliding glass door is blown into the house, frame, and all. We step inside, and it looks like a group of teenagers had a party in the house. Everything is on the floor. Only items in the cabinets are spared.

We try firing up the generator, but the TV is toast. "Well, there goes CNN," I say. Wilson returns with some very nice hunting boots on (My neighbor was always hunting), and Smith barks, "Ok, we need to report in. Get the radio, and let's see if we can find the drone." Wilson heads for the laundry room to get the radio. I turn to Smith and say (Without really being asked), "Really, the radio? The last shit rain of Spheres was not enough to show you they are on to us?"

Smith replied, "Look, Josh, we are here to get eyes on this thing. We have to check in because there is a massive airstrike coming, and, as you know, the recon birds are blind. We have to be able to see the strike and report back the results. But first, we have to know when and where the strike is going to happen."

"Ok then," I said and then continued, "but let's think about this. If they are picking up our signals, they suck at triangulation and at sensors for finding living things. So, let's leverage that and contact the drone from a different location."

Smith looks at me and says - just as Wilson returns with the radio - "Ok Josh, just where do you think we should transmit from?" I answer, "The subdivision behind the house. That way, if or when they come, they will be away from here. And that brings me to the next part of my master plan." Smith looked at Wilson and said, "I'm all ears." We walk back to the Big Ditch, and I show Smith and Wilson something I had noticed last night. I point out next to the stormwater pipe that leads to the street drain in the street above us on the west side of the ditch. The foxes on one side and coyotes on the other side had dug burrows.

And they are not the only ones. The ditch is full of burrows of every description. Finally, I say, "This gentleman is what we need to imitate. The animals seem to have figured out how to avoid these things."

After looking around, some more Wilson says, "I think Josh is right, Sarg." Smith nods and says, "Yeah, we can dig a bunker right up there on the east side of the ditch near the trees. That way, we can have cover going in and out." And so, we set to work. Taking turns, two dug, and the third gathered wood for the support posts, walls, and roof. The Florida sand was easy to dig but was terrible to keep from collapsing on us. But after a day of digging, we had an eight by a ten-foot room that was five feet tall. Not huge, but big enough.

We moved all the weapons, ammo, and gear into the bunker, along with some food and water. The radio was set up at the back of the bunker on a nightstand taken from a neighbor's house, weapons and gear were on shelves from a garage, and the rest of the space was for living. It had some plastic chairs and a small round table. The back of the bunker also held a stroke of genius Wilson had thought up. In my garage, Wilson had spotted a child's toy I had used as a gag in my old life in the cubicles. It is a red plastic periscope. Wilson took that and made an observation hole in the roof. So now we had a way to see out. A Frisbee covered the hole to keep the rains out.

 Smith dug through a bag of gear and pulled out an external antenna for the radio. The antenna had a 21-foot cable attached to it, and Smith slowly inspected every inch. When he was done, Smith said, "We need to find some wire. Copper if we can, and it needs to be 200 feet long or longer with no splices."

 Wilson asked Smith, "Remote transmit site?" "Absolutely," Smith said and then continued, "I think Josh is right in that they don't have the sensors right now to pinpoint where we transmit from. That will most likely change the longer we are here, but I hope this will buy us time."

Wilson asks, "Well, Josh, any suggestion on where to look?" I thought about it. Going over in my mind every house I had been in over the last few weeks looking for food. The problem was I had been looking for food, not wire of any kind. Then it hit me. "Come on!" I said, "I know just where to go, and it's close."

 Smith said, "Not so fast, Josh. How close is it?" I said, "Right the end of the cul-de-sac. Six, maybe seven housetops. He must have been an electrician because he has spools of wire in his garage," Smith continues. "Ok, it's 6 o'clock, and we have not had a Thump all day. The dilemma is, do we go now or wait till the morning?" Wilson added, "Well, on the go side, we have not seen any Spheres today" Smith counters, "The Spheres leave before a Thump, so the fact that we don't see any right now might not necessarily be a good thing. What do you think, Josh?"

 I jump in, happy to be asked for an opinion this time. It makes me feel like part of this team. "From day one with me, it's been all about patterns when it comes to Thumps. This is no different. So, the only pattern we can draw from for where we are at the moment is the day you guys showed up. They let the Thumps rain down and then went right back to a more normal pattern. And I think that is where we are. So, with that said, and knowing there are no guarantees, I say we go right now."

 Smith looks at Wilson, and with a nod, we grab some weapons

and move from the bunker to the garage. A quick check of the golf cart's batteries shows all green. Wilson goes outside to make sure the coast is clear and, in a couple of seconds, gives the all-clear signal of two sharp taps on the side of the garage. I go to open the garage door from the right side, and it won't budge.

Smith looks back from the driver seat of the golf cart and points to the center of the door. The center of the door looks like someone hit it with a blow torch. Some of the panels look almost welded together. Yet, there are no heat marks of any kind. Smith comes over, and together we force the door up just enough to get the cart out. And as we do, the part of the door with the most damage cracks and pieces fall to the ground, making the sound of breaking glass as they hit and shatter on the brick driveway.

Smith and I look at the shards as Wilson joins us from around the side of the garage and comments, "Must have happened when the Spheres were trying to get in" Smith replies, "Right, but what force or energy turns medal into glass?" I ask, "Yet leaves no heat marks?"

Smith cuts off the science class with "Screw it. Let's get this done." And, with that, we are in the cart and moving to the house at full speed. I do not like what I am seeing. There are no animals of any kind. The only sound is the whine of the golf cart electric motor and the wheels crunching pebbles on the blacktop.

The house at the end of the cul-de-sac is just seven doors down but feels like a thousand miles. I point it out to Smith, and we fly into the driveway. Everyone jumps out at once, guns drawn, even Sugar as if to say we have got to make this fast. The house is a wreck. Almost all the windows are shattered, and the roof looks like a rototiller went to work on it. Even the sides of the house have waves going in and out. Smith comments as we move the side door to the garage, "Wow, they really worked this house over," Wilson replies, "Maybe they thought this is where we were?" I add, "I have a theory about that, but it will have to wait till we get back. Let's get the wire and get out here." "Right," Smith grunts as he puts his shoulder into the door, and it groans open.

Smith, Sugar, and I pop in the garage, and just to our left is the wire.

Spools and spools of it. At least 30 different kinds. (Wow, Josh, you were right) Smith says (This guy had to be an electrician to have this much wire.) Smith makes a quick inventory of the spools and then grabs two giant spools. Without a word, I take one, and we are out the door. Wilson says all clear, and we and the wire are in the cart and headed back to my house and safety. I look at Sugar, and she appears relaxed, yet something is not right. There still are no birds, no deer, and no animals of any kind. Smith and Wilson feel it too. They are on high alert with their heads on a swivel looking for danger but finding none.
We pull back into the garage, and I jump out and close the garage door (Or what's left of it) as more parts of it fall off and hit the ground. The daylight streams in through the holes high lighting the dust kicked up by our arrival. We grab our weapons and the wire and move to the bunker.

As we crest the lip of the ditch, we are shocked to be greeted by our friends, the animals! Here they are. More than we have seen before. All the usual ditch goers of Turkeys, Bobcats, Coyotes, Rabbits, Goats, Squirrels, Raccoons, Possums, Chickens, Foxes, Dogs, Cats, and Birds just in greater numbers.

Just like normal, the animals don't care that we are here as we carefully pick our way through them on our way to the bunker. When we get inside the bunker, a pair of Florida panthers and some chickens have made themselves at home. We walk past them and put our gear down as if they are just house pets.

We collapse onto the chairs. No one moves as one of the panthers walks over and sprawls out next to me. Without thinking, I reach down and rub its belly - receiving a loud purr in return.
Wilson looks at me and asks, "Josh, why are all our friends in the ditch, but Sugar did not alert? And why was there no Thump?" I say, "Something has changed. I think it's a good thing Sugar didn't alert because there was no Thump. But with that said, I am right there with you as to why the animals are here. Let's just hope it is something like they are just seeking safety and not some new way those people out there have found to confuse them."

Wilson replied, "Maybe it's just the stress? You know if we are feeling it, they have to be as well" Smith jumped in, saying, "Right, when deer are being hunted, they always go to a sanctuary. Someplace deep in the woods away from people," I say " A good example of something close to this was when the tsunami hit the Indian Ocean; all the animals ran to high ground before the wave and just watched the wave hit. Then when the water receded, they all went back into the jungle."

Just then, as it had so many times before it started. Sugar barked and whimpered, and some foxes ran into the bunker. I said, "Well, I guess we get to see if the bunker works" And at that moment, the Thump came and went. We looked at each other and smiled, knowing we should have gotten down in the ditch the first time just to be safe.

We ate dinner in the bunker that evening as thunderstorms ripped up the sky and rain poured down. By nine o'clock, the storms had passed, and the stars were out. We stepped out of the bunker, climbed out of the ditch, and sat on a fallen oak tree in the back yard next door. I poured some whiskey, and Smith pulled out some cigars. We all had firearms with us, but no one was sure they were of any use.

Smith took a long pull of whiskey and said, "Tomorrow, we string up the antenna. I think we can set it on top of the power pole at the end of the ditch and run the wire back." I said, "Better yet, let's use the pole one down from that one to the east where the poles run towards Publix. That way, it's away from the ditch," Smith puffed his cigar and said as he exhaled, "I like the way you think, Josh" We all laughed.

After a quiet night with no more Thumps, we set out at dawn to install the antenna. We followed the ditch north to its end and then hooked east on the right of way for neighborhood power lines. It had been this way back in the '70s, so the streets did not have power lines.

With only a belt and boots, Wilson climbed right up the pole like a lineman. Once at the top, Wilson glanced around, and not seeing any danger, went to work. He quickly mounted the antenna using a hammer and a few nails and slid down. Smith asked, "See anything?" Wilson replies, "Only a smashed-up neighborhood. They went to town to the southeast. Some places have their roofs caved in. It looks like our part of the hood was let off easy." Smith says, "Ok, let's finish the job at hand."

So, Smith takes the wire from the spool and hooks it to the end of the antenna leads Wilson had run down the pole. A couple of rounds of tape around the connection, and we set out through some woods towards the bunker. We take a pick and shovel and quickly cover the wire a few inches in the Florida sand. I tell Smith and Wilson that we are actually on a huge ancient sand bar that goes for hundreds of feet down. They seem unimpressed by the information.

We run the wire back to the bunker and hook it up to the radio. No sooner does Wilson flip on the power to the radio when it instantly comes to life with a series of beeps. Smith and Wilson look at the display in disbelief. "What?" I ask. Smith starts to read out loud, "Be aware scientists now believe that the energy from the Thump dissipates over time and distance and with this slowdown cover like ditches and pipes no longer provide safety."

A quick look around, and Smith continued, "Scientists also have determined the shape of the Thump to be more egg-like than circular - extending out east and west over the waters of the Gulf of Mexico and the Atlantic." Then Smith started to read more, "You should also be aware that," but stopped. He then took a deep breath and started again, "You should also be aware that what you are now facing is not from this world and that there have been multiple objects confirmed - all impacting along, or close to, the 28th parallel. Two that impacted in North Africa south of Algiers failed to function and have been examined."

Wilson and I look at each other with disbelief as Smith goes on, "Those sites provided dead occupants of the craft and technologies. Including thousands of spheres of the type, you have reported. We are still struggling to understand their capabilities. Early assessments indicate these sites failed because of a lack of water to run the mechanical plants the craft carried. You in central Florida have no such luxury as the groundwater is very close to the surface where you are, and this is where they run the plants from."

Smith went on, "A site in China is running with the same results as you are seeing. The intent of the plants and the beings controlling them is unknown as of the time of the writing of this report. Your

observations to date have been invaluable as you three are without question the only living humans to have survived contact. We will be sending orders soon. Send in your SITREP and rest up. OUT"
Smith punched in a command, and the small beep confirmed the SITREP was sent. He turned to Wilson and me and said, "Welcome to the war of the world's gentlemen."

No sooner had Smith said the words when the bunker and ditch started to fill with animals. The Panthers were first, followed by bobcats and chickens. Sugar started to bark, and cry and all the others joined in this time. The cats were letting out long gut-wrenching sobs, and the chickens were screaming. "Hang on, boys!" I shouted over the din, "It's going to be a long night!"

Just then, the smell hit us. That same acid smell I had smelled the first day. But this time, it was stronger and lingered longer. Then the Thump came. But this one was even stronger than any Thump before - lasting a full three seconds. Not the usual two. Smith said, "Well if there were any doubt they know when we transmit, I'd say that's gone."
I go to the bunker entrance and look outside. What I see next is amazing: 15 or 20 deer come flying into the ditch. I call for Smith and Wilson, "You guys got to see this!" I exclaim, and they rush to the door stepping over and around big cats. Just as they make it to the entrance, some turkeys and sandhill cranes land in the ditch along with other birds and animals. "How can that be!? They should all be dead." Smith asks.

Wilson said it first, "It was stronger! It went over our heads!" And so, we hunkered down for a long afternoon and night, and the Thump makers did not disappoint - pounding out the "New and Improved Thumps or NIT's" as we called them, till around 1 am. Then the Thumps stopped, and within seconds, Spheres flooded the neighborhood.

Wilson raised the periscope up and slowly looked around. He reported what he saw "Lights and more lights. It's like daytime out there. The house blocks most of the view back to the southeast, but the lights are everywhere. Hold on. Uh-oh, lots of light moving up the power line trail. They are right under the antenna. More joining them now. 50

or so. So many I can't count them. Ok, it looks like the herd is moving north."

Wilson's play by play continued, "It looks like three spheres have split off from the herd and are heading our way. They are moving pretty fast." Then we heard a crashing sound followed by tree limbs breaking and hitting the ground. Wilson confirmed what Smith and I thought "Damn, one sphere hit a tree, and it bounced off it like a pinball into one of the other spheres. Then that sphere hit a big old oak tree, and the whole thing came down on top of all three of them."

Wilson kept looking in the direction of the crash, not saying anything till finally Smith could not stand it any longer and asked, "Ok, so what are they doing now?" Wilson replies, "Nothing, the spheres have gone dark," Smith tells Wilson to put on the night vision gear and look. It takes a minute for Wilson to focus but then he seems to have a hard time processing what he is seeing. He pulls back from the periscope and says in a whisper, "One of them popped out of its sphere and ran away to the north. The other two are still there. Sixty feet away tops," his voice trailing off as if they could hear every word.
Smith pushes Wilson out of the way and looks into the night vision goggles. Smith takes in the scene and says in a hushed but business-like tone, "Grab some weapons and follow me." And just like that, he is out the hatch, up and out of the ditch, heading north in the dark with Wilson and me right behind him.

We barely make the woods when three shapes fly past us on the ground. I recognize one as Sugar moving out at full speed. But the other two I can't be sure of - I want to call Sugar back, but I don't want to alert the people in the woods to our presents, so I don't say anything and just keep running.

As soon as we enter the woods, I can see a dim light ahead. We arrive at the light source that is indeed one of three Spheres. Two are dark, but the one, the alien, ran away from is still lighted. Just like the Spheres we saw before, the tan sides of the Sphere are covered with strange brown symbols that slowly change. There is a very low hum coming from the Sphere but no other sounds. The hatch to the Sphere is cracked open with light pouring out from inside. Smith lifts the hatch open and looks inside with his SIG 226 9mm leading the way. Inside are 12 panels with constantly changing shapes on them. Smith says, "Looks like control and coms. But hell, if I can read it. It's all blurry." Wilson looks and ads, "Look at this panel; it looks to be showing location. Like it's for navigation, but it's all wrong."

Now all three of us have our heads crammed in the Sphere, looking at the control panel when movement outside demands our attention. Something is moving in our direction, and it is already dangerously close. The snapping of twigs and shuffling of leaves is only feet away, yet in the dark woods, no one can see a thing.

As one, we turn from the inside of the Sphere and draw our weapons, pointing them in the direction of the sounds coming from the woods. Just as we are about to shoot, Sugar comes into the dim light of the Sphere moving backward, followed by the two Florida panthers. In the low light, we can just make out a dark shape between the three of them.

As they get into the stronger light coming from the open hatch of the Sphere, we get our first look at what our friends have brought us out of the dark woods. It is the alien that had fled the Sphere moments before. It is small, maybe four feet long, with two arms and legs much like ours but with a three-fingered hand with no thumb growing out of each kneecap. A two-inch hook-like horn is coming out of its elbows, pointing down towards its grotesque hands.

The hands on this thing are enormous in comparison to the rest of its body. With six long fingers and two thumbs, all of which look to have eight knuckles. The cats have a hold of the arms, and Sugar has it by the neck, but it is still struggling to get away. And even in the poor light, it is obvious all three of our friends have cuts on them. This thing did not give up easily. Or, more correctly, has still not given up. Smith moves over to the alien and pulls its head back. Its head and face are proportionate to its body. And it has a face only a mother could love. It looks like its face was melted on. Almost flat but with three red eyes blinking back at us.

Smith keeps a grip on its head as Wilson looks the rest of it over. Its uniform is intact - tan with a white V-neck that goes to mid-chest. It also has a thin silver belt that has colors running through it like some kind of code. The colors form packets that then circle the alien again and again.

Smith puts its head back down and says, "Let's get our friend back to the bunker and come back with a camera. HQ is going to love this shit." He no sooner gets the words out when Sugar starts to whimper and cry. Wilson says, Oh, boy, time to go!" I say, "Wait, that's not her Thump cry. Something else is wrong." Looking down at the alien, I see its belt is turning red! Everyone else see's it too. I tell Sugar to "Get up," and with that, she moves towards the bunker with the panthers and the alien in tow. We start moving back to the bunker behind them with Wilson on point.

The alien is going nuts. He, She, It is flailing its arms and legs in an apparent desperate attempt to get away. But the more it struggles, the deeper the panthers and Sugar dig their teeth in - clamping down harder and harder on the alien. And then we hear the first explosion. The explosion lights up the sky to the South of us. Then another and another moving in a huge arch South East before swinging north. Right in our direction! Wilson shouts, "It's the damn Spheres! They are some kind of explosive charge. Hurry!"

As we move back to the bunker, the sky is lit up like day now from the explosions marching right at us—electricity cracks across the sky like waves on the beach. The air smells like sulfur, and the earth shakes. We reach the bunker and dive in behind our friends and the alien.

In the bunker, there is no time to relax. No one is sure the shallow bunker will survive the coming explosion. Smith yells for everyone to brace up against the north wall, and Wilson and I dive over to the wall and wait. Then Wilson points to the alien. Its belt has gone from red to purple. And it has gone completely limp. The explosions rip right up to the Spheres outside and then skip over us - tarting again just to the south of us.

"Wow, that was close," Smith mutters. Wilson continues, "At first, I thought it was an airstrike. You know, one of ours." Smith was shaking the dirt off his uniform, says, "Yeah, me too till about the third or hundredth one. Then I was like, oh shit." I add, "The light show was all I needed to see - it was sci-fi-like shit, man."

Smith says, "Wilson, get the camera and catalog our friend here. Then get on the net and give a SITREP." Wilson takes the pictures, then hooks up the radio and sends the SITREP. Within seconds command responds. "SMITH, YOUR TEAM IS IN DANGER CLOSE PROXIMITY TO ENEMY ACTIVITY IN YOUR AREA. SOURCES HAVE RECORDED EXPLOSIONS NEAR YOU. COMMAND HAS ISSUED A RALLY POINT FOR YOUR TEAM. RALLY POINT SAND IS 2 KICKS SOUTH OF YOUR CURRENT POSITION. WE WILL NEED YOU THERE IN 72 HOURS. MORE DETAILS WILL FOLLOW. GLAD YOU'RE ALIVE. STAY THAT WAY. OUT...
Smith looks at us and says, "Did they even read our SITREP? Did they even have time too? That reply was instantaneous. Well, the good news is we have three days to get our gear together and get ready to move out. But before we do, we will contact command to confirm they want us to move with our friend here."

So, we set a watch and waited for dawn to see what was left outside. That night from the ditch, we could see fires burning all around us to the East, West, and South. But even more alarming was that the animals had not come back to the ditch. Even our panthers had left us. Then it hit me, we had been on the radio, and no Thump had followed. What was going on?

We discuss what could be behind the latest changes, but nothing was for sure. What was certain was we were going where no man had been before in three days. And no amount of talking would change the fact that we just did not have enough knowledge of our adversary. Then Wilson went over to the alien who had not moved for some time. He looked closely at it in the dim light of the bunker and announced it was dead. Smith and I went over and rolled the alien up right off the floor.

As no one was sure how to confirm an alien was dead, I put a light in its face, but it was of no use. We felt all over for some kind of pulse but found none. Wilson was right; the alien was dead. Then Wilson noticed the alien's belt that had been all those different colors in the woods was now dark. "Well," Smith said, "Let's hope it's not a locator beacon of some type, or we are screwed."

Dawn came, and still no animals or Thumps. No one had slept. So we climbed out of the bunker and on top of the ditch. The view was shocking. Damage nearby was total. Homes were almost unrecognizable up and down the street. I wondered what would have happened if the spheres nearest us had exploded. As it was, the spheres sat there like parked cars waiting on their owners to come to pick them up.

We found a large oak tree about one hundred meters from the bunker with a couple of branches hanging down. The limbs had been broken by the force of the explosions. Wilson climbed up the tree and looked around. His report was as expected. "More of the same," Wilson said, "Destruction as far as the eye can see. To the south anyway. Things look better to the North West. I can see homes and trees over there, at least." Wilson climbed down, and we talked about our next move. Smith spoke first, "Let's tell command about the passing of our friend. Then we need to get the golf cart charged up and ready. I want to do this in one move. Two miles is not that far, and with hot batteries, we should be able to cover that in a little over ten minutes' tops. We can use the time we have left to look for a few things like ammo. Some 223 or 5.56 rounds would be great. But let's not get caught out in the open. We still have to worry about those people."

Wilson said, "Right, but from here on till we depart, only one person should go out looking. That will leave the other two here to carry out the mission if something should happen out there."
Smith responds, "No, we stay together. There is only one Sugar, and if something happens to her, the other's mission capabilities will be severely degraded anyway. We made it this far together; we go the rest of the way together."

And. with that, we spent the rest of the day gathering everything we would need for the mission. We got the generator to run and put the golf cart on charge. We moved on foot from house to house that was nearby and picked through the rubble till we had found ammo and food in amounts that made me wonder how we were going to carry it all.

During this time, there was not one Thump. We saw no animals

- not even a bird. It was as if they had all just disappeared. We carried our booty back to the bunker, arriving just at dusk. Wilson entered the bunker first for only a moment before blasting back out the door, exclaiming, "The fucking alien is gone!"

    Smith pushed past Wilson and ran into the bunker only to quickly emerge, saying, "It had all day. It could be anywhere. Let's check the spheres and go from there."

We ran to the top of the ditch and headed north in the woods towards the spheres. It was still dusk, so we had a little light but not enough to see deep into the woods. We had only gone a few feet when a light from the woods flickered and then got brighter.

    Smith said it first, "It's the alien, and it's in the damn sphere!" Then before any else could say another word, the sphere came blasting out of the woods at an incredible rate of speed right at us. The three of us dive out of the way just as the sphere goes by us. We jump up and run to the other two spheres.

    As we get closer, we can see both spheres are pulsing a deep red or maroon color. Wilson blurts out, "This is not good." all three of us slide to a halt, kicking up leaves and dirt as we do so. Smith grabs Wilson and me and says, "Let's go! Grab what gear you can and get in the cart." And so, we race back to the bunker at full speed. Smith is barking out orders as fast as he can, even before we hit the bunker.

    Smith shouts, "Wilson, grab the radio and some weapons. Josh, grab ammo, a rifle, and some food as much as you can run with. I will get the cart ready out front. But whatever you do, do it quickly! Those things are going to blow, and we don't want to be here when they do." The last part went without saying, but it did make me just that much more scared shit less. Wilson and I fly into the bunker. Wilson has the radio disconnected from the antenna wire and on his shoulder in one swift movement. I grab a large backpack full of food, a Ruger Ranch Hand rifle, and two 50 caliber ammo cans full of 223 rounds.

    Wilson and I struggle under the load we carry as we make our way out of the bunker and over the rim of the ditch. And just as we crest the ditch, here come Smith racing at us in the golf cart.
Sugar has been with us this whole time and now leaps into the cart,

followed by Wilson and me. Smith dives the cart like a man chased by the devil. I shout out directions as we make our way out of the hood to Lakelands Highlands Road and hang a right south.

We can't see much because the night is falling, but what little we can see in the headlights does not look good. The hood is a wreck. But it is what we don't see that is the most concerning to me, and that is any wildlife.

We cross Cruise Lake Road and keep going south. We pick up speed as we go downhill. Then I spot what I have been looking for and tell Smith to take the next left.

We drive down a small one-lane road to a house I had seen many times from the road on my way to the preserve to run Sugar. It is a house more at home in New England or Ohio than central Florida. With two stories and a basement garage built into a hillside facing south, it is the last structure before the wastelands to the south. And to the south was where we are headed.

We pulled up to the garage doors, and Wilson jumps out, pulls on the nearest garage door, and nothing happens. He quickly moves to the second one, and with a quick pull, Wala, it opens. Smith drives the cart in, and we move as one to find the best place to survive the next Thump.

Smith finds the door to the basement on the east side and signals for Wilson and me to cover him. We both move to the door and take up positions, one on each side of the door. Without a word, Smith opens the door, and the three of us poor into the next room.
It's empty, but perfect for what we need. With three sides surrounded by dirt facing south, this is the place. We have no night vision gear, so flashlights have to do. We move the supplies from the cart to the basement room when, out of nowhere, the Florida Panthers suddenly appear.

Sugar walks up to greet them, and the three act like old friends. Then the Panthers move to each of us to do the same, rubbing their foreheads on each of us till we did the same to them. Smith had the hardest time with this until Wilson told him, "Just rub your damn forehead with the cats! It will be fine." And it was. All the Panthers wanted was to be welcomed.

IT'S WHAT'S FOR DINNER

As they watched the sunrise from the ridge top, overlooking the valley below, they realized despite their differences, they both saw beauty in the same places.

The cannon fire off to the east had grown closer. They watched the flashes fill the sky with color and sound. They understood the chances of seeing tomorrow were slim but held each other till sleep came - a light fore lone sleep - but sleep, beautiful sleep, just the same. When they woke, the cannon fire had stopped. It had now been replaced with the low sound of heavy machinery moving over open ground in their direction. Having no desire to meet the owners of those machines as one, they picked up the few things they had brought with them and quietly moved deeper into the woods. It was looking like playing for time had only bought them one more night on earth together.

They followed the trail in the woods for the first half a mile - hearing the machines getting louder and closing fast the whole time. Without thinking, he pushed her off the trail down a small slope thick with all forms of brush. He followed, getting to her just as she came to a stop. Landing on top of her, he could feel her heart pounding. They locked eyes as she waited for him to kiss her.

He kissed her long and deeply. He kissed her like it was their last kiss. And she responded with a slow, gentle grinding under him, not wanting the kiss to end. He ended the kiss after what felt like a lifetime and raised his head up slightly. And just as he did, a voice spoke in a whisper, "That was very sweet, but if you two want to live, don't say a word, stay low and follow me.".

They did as they were told and followed the person up the stream that was at the bottom of the bank they had rolled down. They quickly came to an old drainage opening. The person entered the five-foot-high opening and, after a few feet turn left into another tunnel. After ten more feet, they meet a metal door with a lock. Their guide opened the lock and let them in.

They all moved inside and stopped. There was no light whatsoever. Their guide closed the door smartly. She grabbed his arm and turned his body towards their guide. This was not going to end well for anyone.

They could hear their new friend moving around on the other side of the room. Then without warning, there was a click and then light! Everyone tried to get their eyes to adjust to the light. And as they did, it became apparent that their new friend across the room was a woman. And a very attractive one at that. She had already pulled the zipper down on her jumpsuit, exposing a very curvy body. Then she spoke, "First things first."

So, picking up where we left off. In a soft and somewhat sexy voice, the woman who had saved them stepped out of her jumpsuit—and wearing only a bra and panties, laid out the rules. Hi, my name is Layla. As you guys must know, we never talk above a whisper. Even in this bunker, we dare not talk any louder than I am right now. And when we go outside, we always wear jumpsuits to hide our body funk from our visitors. We have food here for three years and water from a spring but enough of that, please tell me your story.

Well, William spoke first. We were on I-4 when the first ship appeared out of nowhere and started firing. And the rest was just a blur of meeting Ona and running as far off the road as they could get. One vibrant memory was of people screaming and being instantly cut down by some invisible force. Ona continued, saying no matter how fast they moved, no matter how well they hid, some new machines came close to killing them. Then after a long pause, William and Ona told the story of how they met some of the beings operating the machines.

Layla was riveted by every word. Ona continued, "We met on I-4 as traffic came to a standstill. After an hour or so, people started getting out of their vehicles. And that's when William I met. We had just finished some small talk when about a mile away, we saw I-4 become an inferno. William grabbed my hand, and we ran. We ran and ran and ran.

For hours, we ran and walked, not knowing why but not stopping till we collapsed. We crossed a small canal at dawn somewhere near Polk City but north of I-4 heading west. We came up over an embankment and to our amazement, spread out before us was one of their encampments!" William went on. "It was massive. It must have taken up 20 acres of real estate. We could see maintenance shops, kitchen buildings, troop tents, fuel depots, and row after row of--------machines." And as his voice trailed off as if seeing all of it again for the first time, Ona said, "And even though the sun was behind us, they knew we were watching and did not care.".

Layla looked at the two young lovers (Yes, they might not know it, but they were lovers, she thought.) and choosing her words slowly and deliberately. "Ok, you two. Time to let you in on a little secret. I, like you, ran for a long time and did see the camps. But most of the camps I saw were of a completely different type. They were more like concentration camps. And our friends behind the machines were packing them full of people.

In the bunker, Layla continued. They spotted me a couple of times but never chased me. I was sure it was my skill at evading and escaping, but it wasn't. I ran right to the edge of a camp, and that is when it happened. Without warning, I could hear their communications in my head. As I looked down, I saw my foot was on a cable running into the camp. If I took my foot off the cable, it stopped. And it was not English at all. It was pictures and sounds that I saw. So long story short, people, they are here for dinner, and humanity is on the menu.

William and Ona were sitting there with their mouths gaped open as Layla continued. "You see, we only have to make it three weeks here. In three weeks, they will leave, and only a hand full of people across the earth will remain." William protested, "What do you mean they will leave? And what about the people? Where is everyone going?" Layla responded, "Away, with them, on the mother ships. The mother ships will be here in a week, and everyone will be processed and taken away. You know, like cattle. Oh, and by the way, this is not the first time they have done this. Oh no, they have been here many times over the millennia. We are just a herd to them. They own us.".

Ona was having none of it. "How can you know this, Layla? You said yourself when you stepped on the cable; it wasn't words or even English." Layla countered, "Right! It was far more than words, and it was meant to be understood by far more than just one race. They have come here with many races or species among them." William chimed in, "Why not take everyone? Why leave a handful behind?" Layla looked at them and, in a cold, emotionless voice, said, "Breed stock. Someone's got to rebuild the herd.".

Ona and William continued with William starting, "Just take us to the cable. We will stand on the cable and see for ourselves what the cable has to say." Ona came in fast and hot "Look, Layla, just tell us what you know. It's painfully obvious to me at least that you are not telling us all you know." Layla just dropped her head and nodded in agreement.

After a long pause, Layla spoke, "Yes, there is more, but I am trying to give you two time to absorb what is going on here. But you want to know, so here we go. They have not only come here to gather the herd; they have been tending to the herd in many ways. They made sure we found high carb processed foods like flour and high sucrose corn sugars. That's right; they have been fattening us up. But you should not have to take my word about all of this. So, let's get dressed and do what I like to call Walking the Cable."

After a long pause, Layla spoke, "Yes, there is more..."

No one said a word as they dressed to Walk the Cable. After putting on the suits, they moved out east towards Polk City. Layla definitely had a knack for moving cross country without being seen. They never moved in a straight line or over open country. But before long, they came to a small ridge. All three, as one peeked up over the last downed tree and below them was a massive camp. Without saying a word, Layla got up and moved a few steps to the south. Ona and William followed. And then, there it was, the cable.

The three walked up the cable and looked down at it from a mere foot away. But already, they could feel a surge of something akin to static electricity pulsing through them. With Layla in between Ona

Short Stories & Fragments from the Other Side

and William, they joined hands without saying a word to each other and stepped on the cable.

The first effect was one of the overwhelming colors and sounds filling their minds. Then out of this wave came Layla's voice.

Layla told them to relax and focus on the colors. Soon she said the pictures would start to come. And come they did. Ona embraced them, and the more she did, the faster the images came to her. But William was having a hard time excepting what his mind was seeing. Still, they pressed on together deeper into the gushing pipeline of data that was the cable.

Just when he thought his mind would explode, William saw a long series of petroglyphs and the meaning of each. He saw what he knew to be Newspaper Rock in Utah. But now, it had become a map of visits and tactics used to corral human beings. At that point, William had one last thought before hitting the ground, "Elvis has left the building."

As William lay on the ground, Ona and Layla continued to ride the cable. Ona saw everything to do with the current invasion. She was getting troop strengths and locations for the whole force, and it was massive. Every spot on the earth, with the exception of Antarctica, having hundreds of thousands of troops, vehicles of every description, and air transports. She also got the current location of the mother ships. And they were close, very close.

Layla felt the power come up from her feet, and this time knowing what to expect, she felt like a pro guiding the two newcomers. She hung back at first, making sure William and Ona were on track before taking a deep dive into the data the cable had to offer. The cable at first tried to direct her into a single subject or time, but Layla would have none of it. She forced her way deeper and deeper into the data, and after what felt like days to her, she found what she so desperately was seeking. It was, she hoped, a way to beat the invasion.

William came to only to find himself still connected to the cable even though his feet were off the cable. He was drowning in data. He could not breathe as his mind fought to disconnect from the cable. He wanted it all just to stop. Stop the memories from thousands of years, but he was in over his head and was just along for the ride. And then, like a dream, he felt Layla and Ona next to him.

William came to with Layla and Ona dragging him back down the hill. Layla yelled at William, "GET UP! GET UP! You have got to start moving!" William got his feet under him and the three-started moving north reversing the way they had come. After a couple of miles, they stopped running and started walking. William looked around and asked Layla, "So Layla, where exactly are we?" Layla didn't miss a beat "We are heading north, staying east of State Road 33, the major north-south road near Polk City. Our guests run up and down 33 constantly, so we can't go too near it, or we will get picked up. It's ok if they see you off in the distance because then it's like you're not worth the effort to go get. We are going back to the bunker that is part of General Van Fleet's home on 33. The older man really knew how to prep for the apocalypse. Too bad he died before it got here."

The trio walked the last mile back to General Van Fleets home, watching the heavy traffic on State Road 33 to the west the whole time. Ona said it first, "The volume, and speed, of the traffic, is definitely saying something." Layla continued, "Yes, they are wide open with the processing right now. The Army and Air Force have been decimated. I saw in the cable MacDill in Tampa put up a good fight along with several

National Guard units from all over. They regrouped around the base, but it was no match. On the plus side, they did take a ton of them with them. Enough that our guests had to bring in reinforcements". William said, "Well, that explains why we have not been hearing any more artillery after day one."

As they approached General Van Fleet's home, Layla signaled for them to get down and follow her. She led them to the south side yard of the house. There, from just inside the wood line, they could see a helicopter landing pad. Layla whispered, "The old man was greeting military helicopters right up to the end5555555555555." Ona said, "What's up with all the satellite dishes and antennas?" Layla said, "I will show you."

So, the trio headed back to the entrance to the bunker behind the house. As they made their way to the main door, they could hear activity all around. Layla said, "We may have overstayed our welcome that close to the road. I should have known better." Ona replied, "It's getting scary the way they totally ignore you and then bang! They want you." William said, "Right, what a crazy place to be."

Then Ona said as they took off the jumpsuits, "They have triggers. You get too close or look like a threat, and you're done. But let's get to the cable. What did we see?" Ona spoke first, "I saw the complete battle plan. And then I saw the logistics to do it. The processing plants are gigantic. People are herded to them and then pushed into a corral or chute. Then, this gigantic plant that is round and pie-shaped swings to the chute. Then the people are pushed in from the chute into the open pie-shaped pen. Once the pen is full, the back of the pen closes, separating it from the chute. Then the packed pen has an acid-like fluid poured over them from above. Instantly all the clothing and hair melt off the people in the pen. Next, as on cue, the people defecate as one, and a warm shower of water pours over them, leaving them clean and naked. Without warning, the top of the pen near the center opens, and a whirling sound coming from it is next. People from the back start to scream as the back wall pushes them towards the front, and the people in front see what awaits them. It is a wall of blades. A food pressor on a huge scale. As people get pushed in, they are instantly turned to a cloud of vapor."

Ona continued in a matter of fact tone, "And then, off to one side is a large pipe that sprays what is unusable into the drainage. The discharge is made up mostly of teeth and hard bone, along with things like dental and breast implants. But you also get hip and knee replacements. They make no attempt to recover or recycle these metals. When the pile gets too big, a few machines come out and knock it out of the way. And then there are the pullers of the prime cuts department. They are seven feet tall, leather-skinned, with four muscular arms. They have no hair or ears; you can see and wear a muzzle around their large mouths with goggles over their eyes. I took from the muzzles they would snack too much without it. So, anyway, the wheel turns, the gate opens, and the pullers plow into the crowd. They quickly pull out the people they need depending on the order they are filling. Sometimes it's lean cuts, sometimes fatty cuts. But the process is the same. The puller pushes the chosen one back to the open pie-shaped pen. Only this pen does not open at the end. No, this one stops at a line of tables and racks. Once the door to the chute closes, the pullers get to work. They take carving tools and dismantle people alive. The puller is holding the person with one set of arms and taking them apart with the other. Mostly they gut them first, but sometimes they like to play with the victim first. And they are not against raping their victim first. Oh, men and women are treated equally here. But they always get back to work deboning meat and packaging it very precisely. When the order is filled, the boxes are loaded on a tram and taken to storage. And they do this 24/7."

BUNKER LIFE

Episode One: Bring Out Your Dead!
Chris dresses up in a brown robe with a bell and walks around his and Jeanette's over 55 community yelling, Bring Out Your Dead! This does not go over well with other residents.

Episode Two: Looking for A Hug
In this episode, a fevered Jeanette goes out looking for a hug. Mayhem ensues as people scatter to escape.

Episode Three: Looking for Friends.
Chris and Jeanette, desperate for new faces, invite some neighbors into the Bunker that they have started to call Hotel California.

Episode Four: Came in Like A Wrecking Ball.
When Chris finds a huge PPE stash, Jeanette must step in to try and make him do the right thing.

Episode Five: The Show Must Go On!
Chris recruits his neighbors to put on a safe social distance variety show. Things quickly degenerate into an over 55, alcohol-fueled, burlesque stripper show.

Episode Six: Getting Over the Hump!
When the internet breaks, Chris digs up the cables coming into the over 55 hood to fix them. But when he digs up the power lines by mistake, the bright flash in the night sky plunges the hood into darkness. Jeanette tells everyone it's COVID 19's fault.

Episode Seven: Courage Is Free.
When the truth is found to be lies, courage is found in the most unexpected of people.

Episode Eight: The Experiment.
Jeanette finds a casino bus parked and running in the over 55 hood. So

she does what anyone would and drives around the hood picking up people. It's not long before the people on the bus know this trip is not what they thought!

Episode Nine: Info Wars.
As information becomes the new currency, Chris and Jeanette accuse each other of hoarding. Even going so far as to say, "You are keeping that from me for some sick, evil, or deceitful trickery."

Episode Ten: Parking Wars.
After receiving a tip about out of state people flooding the hood, Chris and Jeanette take action. They cruse the over 55 hood and find out of state car tags. The problem is, neither one is willing to risk infection to confront the invaders. CheckMate!

Episode Eleven: Palm Tree Radio.
As the days blur into weeks, Chris takes palm tree branches to make a radio to talk to Moscow. Everyone thinks Chris is just doing yard work. But that changes when the Humvee's roll in from the MacDill Air Force base in Tampa.

Episode Twelve: When the Bra's Come Off.
It started small - a simple challenge, made out of boredom, to set the puppies free. It ends with news helicopters circling the over 55 hood.

Episode Thirteen: Bang A Gong.
As the helicopters circle overhead, the residents, driven by boredom, morph the puppies' protest into a 1960's style hippie fest. The ensuing footage from the news helicopters is deemed too inappropriate for TV by all the networks.

Episode Fourteen: Teach Your Children Well.
Just as the night of the long togas dies down, the word gets out. It's a party! And people start to flood the over 55 hood looking for a good time.

Episode 15: The Passing.
And just like the virus will in time, the party burned itself out. People went home and left the hood a mess. Trash was everywhere. Somewhere the sounds of Eric Clapton's Layla could be heard blaring from a stereo, but it was done. Life went on.

Episode 16: Truth Teller.
Chris goes around the hood to tell all that will listen to him and his vision of what is to come. He tells them before the pandemic is over, swarms of flying monkeys will eat all the locusts' swarms around the world. Then the flying monkeys will turn on the humans - biting, killing, and pooping everywhere. Especially pooping on cars (mostly Fords), they will love to poop on cars. Then, in early summer, hurricanes will come and blow the flying monkeys away. Cleaning up the poop as the storms pass by. Not all are ready to hear the words of the profits, but time will tell. Many go back and clean shotguns in hopes of a new protein source that will supplement the meat shortage at the grocery stores.

Episode 17: Death Race 2020.
With not much to do, Chris organizes a Golf Cart race in the over 55 hood. Things rapidly go downhill, as many in the race take it as an opportunity to settle old scores—the number of ambulances needed to tend to the injured quickly outpaced what was available. The buzz of news helicopters overhead is just a normal thing by now. The injured will give interviews, and the rest, as they say, is history.

Episode 18: Greetings.
Chris's new greeting, "How's your apocalypse going?" goes viral in many ways.

Episode 19: Chris wakes from the COVID-19 dream.
The outbreak never happened!

ABOUT THE AUTHOR

Chris Ammann was born in Connecticut and grew up on Long Island Sound in the 70s, where he and his friends, brothers, and sister spent the summers fishing, swimming, and running deep into the woods. It was in the woods where, as kids, they would tell each other ghost stories.

These days he lives in Tampa, Florida, and is a book and short story writer specializing in outside-the-box sci-fi with plenty of thrillers and suspense. He has found a way to take a normal situation and twist it until all the reader can do is buckle up and go along for the ride.

Follow him on Facebook @alookinsidemymind (A Look Inside My Mind).